You are cordially invited to Blythe Gifford's

Royal Weddings

A hint of scandal this way comes!

Anne of Stamford, Lady Cecily and
Lady Valerie serve the highest ladies
in the land. And with their close proximity
to the royal family they are privy to
some of the greatest scandals the royal court
has ever known!

As Anne, Cecily and Valerie's worlds threaten
to come crashing down three men enter their
lives—dashing, gorgeous, and bringing with
them more danger than ever before. Suddenly
these three strong women must face a new
challenge: resisting the power of seduction!

Follow Anne of Stamford's story in
Secrets at Court

Read Cecily, Countess of Losford's story in
Whispers at Court

Discover Lady Valerie of Florham's story in
Rumours at Court

All available now!

D0494589

Author Note

The monarchies of medieval Europe were a small, elite society. Kings and their families were expected to marry partners of similar stature, and such royal marriages were not expected to be love matches. They were arranged, like most medieval marriages, for reasons dynastic or financial, as heartless as a business transaction.

Even when countries were at war a marriage between royal families could create alliances, cement peace, or allow another ruler's family the right to a distant throne.

But love has a way of interfering with such logical plans—for royals *and* for their subjects…

RUMOURS AT COURT

Blythe Gifford

Published in Great Britain 2017
by Mills & Boon, an imprint of HarperCollins*Publishers*
1 London Bridge Street, London, SE1 9GF

© 2017 Wendy B. Gifford

ISBN: 978-0-263-92579-1

Printed and bound in Spain
by CPI, Barcelona

After many years in public relations, advertising and marketing, award-winning author **Blythe Gifford** started writing seriously after a corporate lay-off. Ten years later she became an overnight success when she sold her Romance Writers of America Golden Heart® finalist manuscript to Mills & Boon. Her books, set primarily in medieval England or early-Tudor Scotland, usually incorporate real historical events and characters. The *Chicago Tribune* has called her work 'the perfect balance between history and romance'.

She loves to have visitors at blythegifford.com, facebook.com/BlytheGifford and Tweets at twitter.com/BlytheGifford.

Books by Blythe Gifford

Mills & Boon Historical Romance

Royal Weddings

Secrets at Court
Whispers at Court
Rumours at Court

The Brunson Clan

Return of the Border Warrior
Captive of the Border Lord
Taken by the Border Rebel

Linked by Character

A Yuletide Invitation
'The Harlot's Daughter'
In the Master's Bed

Stand-Alone Novels

The Knave and the Maiden
Innocence Unveiled
His Border Bride

Visit the Author Profile page at millsandboon.co.uk.

For my editor, Linda Fildew,
whose constant patience and support
has made this journey possible.

Acknowledgement

Many, many thanks to author Deborah Kinnard,
who dropped everything to double-check
my Spanish translations.
I owe you, friend!

Chapter One

London—February 9th, 1372

Despite the cold, it seemed all of London had turned out to gawk at the Queen and to see the Duke of Lancaster, or 'My Lord of Spain" as he now preferred, stand before them for the first time as King of Castile.

Sir Gilbert Wolford stood beside the man as he prepared to welcome his new wife, the titular Queen of Castile, to his grand palace on the Thames. A sense of unease threatened the triumph of the day. This was a celebration, yes, but of a battle far from won.

The English Parliament had accepted Lancaster, the son of England's King, as the rightful Lord of Castile. Many Castilians, including the current King, disagreed.

But some day, Gil would return to the Iberian plains at Lancaster's side. This time, he would not stop until they stood, triumphant, in the Palace of Alcázar. The token he had carried since their first attempt weighed heavily in his pocket—his promise to himself.

Gil spared a glance for the ladies gathered to greet the Queen. Lady Valerie, Scargill's widow, stood among them. She had just come to court and they had not met, but she had been pointed out to him from afar, easy to find in her widow's wimple, covered as completely as a nun.

He had a last duty to perform for her dead husband.

One he would rather avoid.

In Castile, Gil had been known by the enemy as *El Lobo*, The Wolf, because he would kill to protect his men. But no man could save them all. Not in war. He had not been able to save Scargill and now the man's widow must bear the price.

The procession stopped before the palace. The event had been arranged as if the Queen were newly come, as if she and her husband had never met. In truth, they had married on the Continent months before so as to lose no time in creating an heir.

A son.

Gil resisted regret. At thirty, he had no wife, no son and no prospect of either. Nor would he until he could leave this island and his family's past well and truly behind. *El Lobo* was a byname more flattering than the ones they called his family here in England.

The Queen's litter was carried up the stairs, lurching from side to side until it reached the landing where the Duke stood. Then it was lowered and Constanza, the Queen, stepped out to approach her husband.

Accustomed to the heat of the Spanish plains, neither the Queen nor her retinue had arrived with cloaks to fight the British cold. Wearing borrowed mantles, unmatched and ill fitting, they looked every bit the court in exile.

Yet the Queen without a kingdom did not act humbled. Her husband John of Gaunt might be Duke of Lancaster and son of the English King, but he could call himself King of Castile only because she was his wife. It was *her* father, *her* blood that carried the right to rule.

Now, within sight of her husband, she nodded to an attendant who removed the cloak.

Behind him, the women of the household gasped.

The Queen's red-velvet gown, bright as blood, drew every eye. She stepped towards her husband, slowly, with only slight deference. A mere inclination of the head. Barely a bend to the knee. Proud, young. At seventeen, little more than half her husband's age.

Comely enough, Gil supposed. But no woman would ever replace the man's dead Duchess. With her, he had found not only a dynastic partner, he had found love of the kind the troubadours celebrated. Could a man expect that twice?

Gil did not expect it at all.

And yet, in his dreams, he imagined standing in the peaceful gardens of Alcázar with a woman who gazed at him, eyes full of love…

Only a dream. Now was not the time for a wife, who, like the Lady Valerie, might too soon become a widow. Before he took a bride, he would be a new man in a new place, miles and years away from his tainted past.

He brought his mind back to the present day and passed to the Duke the velvet sack which held the wedding gift to Constanza. With two hands and proper ceremony, Lancaster presented his offering, but instead of taking it, she left him with arms outstretched, not reaching for it.

A slight so obvious that, instead of murmurs, the air carried only shocked silence.

Gil hoped she had hesitated for fear her fingers were too cold to hold it safely.

Finally, she nodded to the man next to her. With one hand, he grasped the bottom of the bag while, with the other, he pushed it aside to reveal a gold cup, carved like a rose, covered with a lid featuring a dove in flight.

It was one of the most beautiful creations of a man's hand that Gil had ever seen.

But the lady did not smile to see it. Instead, she waved it away to be cared for by one of her attendants.

Gil gritted his teeth, frowning. The woman should be more grateful. If the Duke had not come to her rescue, she and her sister would still be homeless, orphaned exiles in France. Only with her husband's help did she have any hope of regaining the life and title she had been born to.

The Queen motioned to one of her counsellors, a heavy-set Castilian priest with a wide forehead, who stepped forward and began to speak.

'La Reina asks me to say she is happy to greet her husband, Monseigneur d'Espagne.'

Halting English, Gil thought, but better

than that of the Queen, who, he understood, spoke little but Castilian.

'Tell Her Grace,' John said, looking at Constanza, 'that I welcome her to London.'

Another whispered conference. The woman's lips thinned and she spoke sharply to the priest.

He cleared his throat and faced his 'King' again.

'La Reina says that she hopes her stay here is brief. She expects you to return to her homeland and restore her throne before the year is out. Until she goes home to Castile, she asks that I give you all assistance to administer the state and plan for battle.'

Now, it was the smile of the Duke, 'My Lord of Spain', that turned thin and hard.

Gil's expression mirrored his lord's. Yes, Lancaster was King because he had married the Queen, but he *was* the King. And the King, not some Castilian priest, would be the one to select his military advisers. Gil expected to be among them.

'Thank the Queen for me,' Lancaster said. 'I welcome your help.'

Only a courtesy, Gil thought, holding back a protest as the Queen's younger sister and other members of her retinue hurried towards the warmth of Lancaster's palace. The Duke could not refuse a wife's request, no matter how rude, before a crowd. Nothing had changed. When the time came for war, he would rely on Gil and his other long-time companions.

As they turned to follow the women, he put the worry aside. He had another duty today.

The ladies of the court clustered around the doors, waiting to enter, and he looked for the Lady Valerie, pausing to study her, as he would assess the terrain before beginning an assault.

At first glance, he saw nothing remarkable. Swathed in her wimple and weeds, facing away from him, she was shorter than the other women. Was she fair or dark? Were her features pleasant to look on? Had her husband smiled when he came to her bed?

A gust of wind found her cloak. She reached to battle it, stopping his inappropriate imaginings. He should not think thus of the widow of one of his men.

She knew of her husband's death, of course. That had happened months ago and she had been informed, so she would not first hear the news from him. For that, he was grateful.

But the ragged scrap of white silk that the

man had tucked against his heart—that, at least, deserved to find its home again.

The wind subsided. She looked up and he caught a glimpse of her face. The woman had sad, dark eyes. Perhaps the return of the token her husband had cherished would give her comfort.

The English and Castilian ladies were shepherded into the palace and then to the Hall side by side, close enough for Valerie to hear the foreign chatter. She could not follow all the words, but the lilt of the language, the faint scent of Castilian soap, seemed familiar.

Perhaps her blood remembered these things. Blood that had come from another Castilian woman exiled to England, generations ago. Like Constanza, Queen of Castile, she, too, had been taken from her home and sent to a distant place.

Valerie touched the brooch of copper and enamel on her gown, a reminder of her long-dead relative. She must hold her head high amidst the unfamiliar trappings of court. Soon enough, she would be allowed to return to the earth of her home and her garden, slumbering now in winter.

The Queen reached the front of the Hall

and turned to face the room. Valerie squinted, trying to see her clearly. She was fair, even sallow. Were her eyes blue? Too far to see, but her nose looked longish for the fashion, her figure tall and sturdy.

Her looks, in truth, were unimportant. Her gift to her husband was her country, not her beauty. And a woman, even a royal one, had no more choices than any other woman. She must marry for reasons of state, no matter what her heart. And if she wanted to be Queen in fact instead of just in name, this woman needed a man both willing and wealthy enough to fight for her kingdom.

Suddenly, the Queen touched a hand to her belly and the curtain of women around her closed tightly.

Were the rumours true? The Queen had arrived in England months ago, but had stayed in the country, some said because of the early ills of being with child.

The Duke—Valerie could still not think of him as a king—would have wasted no time getting an heir on her. They both needed to prove they could produce another generation to sit on Castile's throne, so that might be the reason the woman did not look her best. All would be forgiven if she bore a son.

Something Valerie had failed to do.

'She looks so young,' Lady Katherine, next to her, whispered.

Valerie murmured something that might be mistaken for assent. The Queen was nearly Valerie's own age and only a few years younger than Lady Katherine. Katherine, too, was newly widowed and had three children of her own. She might be feeling the length of her life.

Though she mourns her husband no more than I do mine.

She could not say how she knew. They had met only recently and never spoken of it, but Valerie felt certain that they both re-cited the requisite prayers for the loss of a husband while secretly revelling in their new freedom.

The line of ladies shielding the Queen parted. The Queen had settled into a chair at the front of the hall beside the Duke. Her sister came to stand beside her and the pro-cession of lords and ladies shuffled into line to be presented.

Valerie, following Katherine, was surprised and honoured that she had been invited to this ceremony. Her husband had been a knight, but a lowly one. Lady Katherine's husband had been the same, but she was here because she took care of the Duke's children by his first wife. Now, she would move into his second wife's household, a strong link to what the Queen needed to know about England and, perhaps, even about her husband.

As Valerie was presented to at least a dozen of the Queen's ladies, she was called upon to do little beyond nod politely. The Queen's people smiled, silent, not attempting the unfamiliar tongue.

Even the Queen remained impassive in the face of all the introductions. Surely the poor woman had absorbed nothing about the strangers paraded before her.

Then, Valerie heard her name called and knelt before the Queen. A flurry of conversation, the Duke, speaking to the interpreter, who then spoke to the Queen.

Descended from one who came to England with Eleanor of Castile, wife of the first Edward.

Ah, it was her ancestor who had brought her here, the woman who had served that other foreign Queen nearly a hundred years ago.

Finally, the Queen understood and nodded. *'Habla la lengua de sus antepasados?'*

Now she was the one who struggled to understand. Speak? Did she speak...?

She was a widow now. She could speak aloud, even to a queen, without looking over her shoulder for her husband's permission. And yet, the language of Castile was as foreign to her as hers was to the Queen.

She shook her head. 'Only enough to say *Bienvenida.*' That meant welcome. At least, she thought it did.

It was enough to make the Queen smile. *'Gracias.'* She stretched out a hand, touching the brooch with reverent fingers, then spoke to her interpreter.

'La Reina wishes to know, is the brooch you wear hers?'

Valerie smiled. 'Yes, Your Grace. It, too, came from Castile.' The Queen, the story went, had been generous to her ladies.

Nodding, this Queen cleared her throat and spoke, each word careful and distinct. 'We to meet again.'

The words touched her like a benediction. 'I hope so, Your Grace.'

Valerie paused to kneel before the Duke— no, the King—barely looking at him as she hugged the Queen's words close to her heart.

When she rose, still smiling, and turned

away, it was to come face to face with the knight she had seen earlier at the Duke's right hand. Dark, ragged brows shielded pale blue eyes. His nose and cheeks were sharply carved. He looked to be a man, like her husband, more at home in battle than in the Hall.

She nodded, courteous. Waiting.

'Lady Valerie, I am Sir Gilbert Wolford.'

Her momentary glow faded. 'The man they call The Wolf.'

The one who had commanded her husband to his death.

When Lady Valerie turned to meet his eyes, for a moment he could not speak.

Now he could see her plainly. Fair skin. Dark eyes that changed expression when she knew him for who he was. Was it his family history or his reputation in battle that erased both smile and sadness? No matter. Now, he faced a strong, impenetrable shield, through which he could glimpse no emotion at all. Until then, he would have judged her a woman who needed protection. Now, he thought she would have been an asset on the battlefield. 'Some have called me that,' he answered, finally.

An awkward silence. 'What do you want of me?' she said, finally.

The time had come. 'Your husband served in my company.'

She glanced down at the floor. 'I know.' Had her sadness returned? Would there be tears?

He hurried to speak. 'Then you know that the siege was broken by that attack. That his death was not in vain.'

'That is a comfort, surely.' Her tone suggested otherwise.

'He was a worthy fighter. His death was a blow.'

Now her gaze met his again. Her shield had not slipped. 'More so to me.'

Ah, then she blamed him for the man's death. She had the right. 'Men die in war, no matter what we do.' War was not what those at home imagined. It was not...glorious.

He pulled the stained, crumpled silk from his tunic. 'Your husband was carrying this when he died. I thought to return it to you so you would know he treasured the thought of his wife.' He waved it in her direction. A poor, limp thing, even more wrinkled and dirty now than it had been when he took it from the man's body.

She did not reach for it. Instead, she recoiled, as if it were a live thing with teeth.

He shook his outstretched hand, wishing to free himself of it. 'Do you not want it back?'

'Back?' The word, barely a whisper. Then, she lifted that hard, impenetrable gaze and met his eyes again. 'It was never mine.'

Chapter Two

Valerie closed her eyes, blocking the sight of the muddy, wrinkled piece of cloth. It was proof, proof again, of how little she had mattered to her husband.

Sir Ralph Scargill had sailed away to war in the springtime. Another spring came and went. She had not missed him. Though she knew the war was going badly, no one bothered to report details to a knight's wife and he was not a man to send home tender words.

So it was only a few months ago, when the Duke returned and her husband did not, that she knew the whole of it. Or thought she did.

For now, this man, the one they called The Wolf, stood before her with furrowed brow and an outstretched hand, holding silk that had touched the flesh of an unknown woman who had, no doubt, lain with her husband.

Had she, too, had to hide her bruises?

Even if that were true, he must have cared for this woman to carry a reminder of her into battle. He had never asked Valerie for a token.

And she had never offered one.

But the man before her, a hardened warrior, blinked to hear the truth. 'I thought…'

She felt a twinge of regret. Poor man. He had only tried to comfort a grieving widow, not knowing she had never grieved.

A frown touched his brows and she saw compassion in his eyes. Around them, people had stopped to look.

She turned away, abruptly, and heard the murmur of conversation again. Bad enough to have seen the man's shock. She did not want to face his pity. Or anyone else's.

'Wait.' The word low and urgent. His fingers circled her wrist, a touch at once hard and hot.

Reluctantly, she looked back. 'Why?' The scrap of silk, discarded, now lay crumpled at his feet. She resisted the urge to step on it.

'I'm sorry,' he said.

Sorry for her, he meant. Sorry he had embarrassed the poor, wronged widow.

A smile to appease him. A man must never be made to feel uncomfortable. 'What my husband did was not unusual.' Though usually not spoken aloud. 'And not your fault.'

'Forcing the knowledge on you was. I supposed at the truth and rode ahead. A mistake a commander should never make.'

She covered his hand with hers, intending to lift it from her arm. Instead, her palm lingered, tempted by the warmth of his skin.

Her husband's hands had been cold. Always cold…

She let go, quickly. So did he. 'I'm sure you are a good commander and did all you could. Now, please. I must…'

She could not say more. She only knew she must flee this man and all the certainty he brought. Even she could see that the well-worn scrap of cloth was silk, a costly material. Had she been a high-born woman? Or had he bought her something precious and rare? Either way, it had been sacrificed so that he could carry a reminder of this woman into battle.

Searching the hall for a familiar face, she returned to Lady Katherine's side, hoping there would be no questions about what The Wolf had wanted of her.

But her companion's attention was on the Duke, who was leaving the dais as the final presentations had been made. She murmured a greeting to Valerie, but did not turn her head, her gaze on the man with something like longing. She looked at him as if…

Valerie shook off the thought. Just because she knew the truth about *her* husband, she was seeing adultery all around her. No doubt it was there. All men looked for passion outside the marriage bed. A wife must expect no more than duty. She had not expected fidelity from Scargill, but she had never thought to have his infidelities displayed openly to all.

'Come,' Lady Katherine said, 'I want to speak to the Duke about the children.' A pause and blush. 'I mean,' she said, with a lift of her chin, 'to Monseigneur d'Espagne.'

My Lord of Spain. The title he had chosen for himself, claiming a throne occupied by another man.

But that fact was firmly ignored today. Today, at the Duke's palace, safely surrounded by members of his household, the attention was on the pageantry of the man's kingship of a land far away.

As they approached, Lancaster's smile was all for Katherine. Valerie was invisible in her wake.

'How are you?' And then, noticing Valerie, his tone shifted. 'And how are the children?'

'The girls are biddable and even tempered. And young Henry thinks he is ready to be a knight though he is barely five.'

Lancaster chuckled. 'He lacks patience.' The lack did not seem to disturb his father.

Katherine turned to Valerie. 'You know Lady Valerie.'

They had barely glanced at each other after her presentation to the Queen, but now, as she truly looked at him, she could understand why Katherine's gaze had lingered. Strong, tall, a warrior, yes, but a man one might trust in peace as well. Perhaps he would make a good king for those people in far-off Castile.

'Your husband was a brave man,' he said.

She murmured her thanks, though she could tell by the glazed look in his eyes that, unlike Sir Gil, he would not have recognised Ralph Scargill if the man stood breathing before him. Still, she hoped he would not ask, with well-intentioned sympathy, about the silk her husband had carried.

He did not. 'The Queen smiled when she met you,' the Duke continued. 'There are few here that she…likes.'

Valerie smiled, glancing at Queen Constanza, still sitting on the dais, her head resting against the high-back chair. Her eyes were closed. Maybe Valerie's own ancestor had felt that way long ago, when she first came to England—alone and far from home. 'Perhaps my connection to her country was a comfort, Your Grace.'

'What word do you hear from your steward?' Lancaster was, apparently, done with the topic of his wife.

Now Valerie smiled, thinking of Florham. Home. The one corner of the world that was her own. 'All was well when I left.' How soon could she return? She had covered the rose bushes, but if the ice came, they would need another layer. 'We have food enough in storage for the winter and we have a new plan for the rye fields...'

His gaze drifted and she bit her tongue. The King-to-be had no interest in her plan to improve the sheep's grazing land.

'You will not need to worry about such things much longer. It is time I chose a new husband for you.'

Forgetting all, she gripped his arm. 'But I only learned of my husband's death a few months ago. I need no help with the land.' She stumbled over words, trying to make it right

with the Duke. 'By the time the quince tree
buds, I had hoped—'

There was stunned shock on his face and
on Lady Katherine's.

She let go of his arm and lowered her eyes.
How quickly she had forgotten. She could
not speak so to any man, least of all to this
one.

'What, exactly, had you hoped?' the Duke
said, his smile turning sour.

'I had hoped, my lord, to have a year to
mourn.' A year of freedom, to be left in peace
in her beloved garden, beyond a man's beck
and call.

But as she looked at Lancaster's face, it
dawned on her, as it should have done when
she first heard of her husband's death: he had
been promised forty marks per year in war,
twenty marks per year in peace. For life.

And that life was now over.

His expression gentled. 'I understand your
sorrow, Lady Valerie, but you have no children.'

'Of course, yes, I know,' she murmured.
And she did. She must be given to a new husband, a new protector, a new man to be en-
dured. And some day, no doubt, she would find
evidence of a new malkin defiling her bed.

At least the land was her own, beyond a husband's reach.

'Besides,' he asked, in a tone that did not seek an answer, 'what else could you do?'

'Perhaps, my lord, I had thought...' She paused, not knowing how the sentence would end. She could not tell him what she really wanted. My Lord of Spain cared nothing for her garden.

But he had mentioned his Queen. Perhaps that...

'I had thought,' she said, 'that I might be of service to the Queen. For a time.'

He looked puzzled. 'Service?' Lancaster asked. 'In what way?'

How could she answer? Certainly the Queen did not need a lady gardener in her retinue. Valerie turned to Lady Katherine and raised her brows, an appeal for help.

'I might be of help to Lady Katherine.' The woman had his children and her own to manage, as well as her duty to the Queen.

He waved his hand, a gesture of dismissal. 'The Queen has a bevy of her own ladies from Castile.'

Valerie put a hand on Katherine's arm and squeezed. 'That is certainly true, but none of them can help her learn of England. Certainly

Lady Katherine will do that, but I thought my connection to her country would be a comfort. And Lady Katherine will be so busy with the children...'

Please. Would Katherine understand her plea? Could she sway the Duke?

She could only pray that another woman would understand her meaning.

'What a good idea, my lord,' Katherine said, patting Valerie's hand and turning her smile on Lancaster. 'Lady Valerie could be another companion to the Queen as she adjusts to life here. And perhaps help me with your children as well.'

Valerie nodded, hiding her dismay. She knew less of children than of the court. The Queen's momentary approval had warmed her, but a few remembered Castilian words would not make her fit company for royalty. She had wanted to return to the earth of Kent, not be stranded here in London.

Still, if it would delay the time when she must be sent to warm another man's bed, at least for a while, she would do it. 'Yes, I would be happy to be of help.'

The man's scowl had not completely faded.

Now she must don the obedient smile, the one that made a man feel powerful and generous. 'Of course, the choice is yours, my lord. I shall do as you wish and be grateful for your kind consideration.' The words sounded wooden, even to her ears.

He smiled, finally, as if a servant had cleaned up after a guest who had clumsily dropped a goblet. 'I am certain that Katherine will be glad of your help.'

'As will the Queen, of course,' Katherine added hastily.

And Valerie, who was certain of no such thing, dipped and murmured her thanks. Katherine put an arm around her shoulders and Valerie struggled to stay calm as Katherine led her away. A few more weeks, then, when she could move and speak without a husband's approval. 'Thank you,' she said, when they were out of earshot. 'I cannot yet bear...'

She shook her head and let the words go. She had said too much already.

'Do not expect a long reprieve,' Katherine said, patting her shoulder. 'No later than spring, I would think.'

She looked at Katherine, unable to hide her dismay. In March, she had hoped to be weeding the earth around the quince tree. 'Has he chosen *your* husband?' She could not keep the bitter edge from her question. Katherine was also a widow. Surely she, too, would be given as a prize to some man.

'No.' Katherine looked away, a flush of colour on her cheeks. 'The Duke has been kind to allow me to help his wife and with his children.'

'I wish I could remain unmarried, as you are.'

'Perhaps I shall marry again…some day.' There was a strange yearning in the woman's words.

Perhaps Valerie had been wrong. Perhaps Katherine had loved her husband deeply and longed for another union. 'My marriage was not something I want to repeat.' A difficult admission. One Valerie should not have made.

'All are not so. The Duke and the Lady Blanche loved each other very much.' Wistful. As if such a thing where possible.

One marriage out of how many? More than the waves on the sea. She shook her head. 'I have not seen a marriage like that.' Certainly not between her own mother and any of her husbands.

And yet, a woman had no other choice. She could marry herself to God or to a man. For some widows, wealthy ones, a husband's death could mean a new life of independence. She would not be one of them.

She had the land, yes, the earth that had been handed down since that long-ago woman came from Castile: that, at least, would always be hers. It might even have been enough that she could have been left alone, to tend her roses and her quince tree. The very thought was a glimpse of freedom.

Instead, she would be given to a new gaoler whose every whim she would be forced to obey. She knew that. Had always known it. Yet just for a moment, she had hoped for a different life. 'But you have found another path—'

Katherine touched her arm. 'Do not seek to trade your life for mine. There are things you do not know.'

She dropped her arm and turned away, and Valerie wondered of the things she did not know. Well, she would allow Katherine her secrets. There were things she, too, did not wish to share.

But why should Katherine be left free with her children when she—?

Ah. Of course. It was because of the children. Katherine had three children. Valerie had none, so she must be given to yet another man. She must take him to her bed, over and over, until his seed took root and she carried his child.

What if she failed again?

Snatching the discarded silk from the floor, Gil wondered what Scargill had been thinking of, as his life slipped away. Of the battles in Gascony? Of the woman who last warmed his bed?

Or had he been praying to God to forgive the wrongs he had done to the wife he had left behind?

Gil tucked the silk scrap into his tunic. He would drop it in the rubble later.

Now, he looked around the Hall. A waste of time, all the trappings of this fantastical court. A fraud and a distraction for a man who should be worried about holding the land instead of the title.

He has taken a bride who has made him a king. But he still must take the throne.

John, Duke of Lancaster, King of Castile, Monseigneur d'Espagne, was tall and strong and handsome, as if he were King in fact. At thirty-two, barely older than Gil, the man was in his very prime. No man in England, perhaps no man in Christendom, had more personal wealth.

But this man was the son of Edward, King of England, so nothing short of kingship could ever be enough.

Had he been the first son, the English throne would have been his, but his father the King had spawned many worthy sons, so to grasp the throne he desired, Lancaster had been forced to look beyond the island.

Gil shared the man's hunger to leave England. Castile was his answer, too, the place he could prove himself the man he wanted to be.

But tonight, instead of organising his invasion plan, Lancaster was wandering the hall, King of Castile only because he had married the dead King's daughter.

It would take a war, not just a marriage, to win the throne.

Gil hung back, reluctant to interrupt Lancaster's conversation with the Ladies Katherine and Valerie, but when they stepped away, he came to Lancaster's side. His gaze followed the small woman, cloaked in black. Had she mentioned that he had flaunted her husband's indiscretion in her face?

'She should be married,' Gil said, vaguely

feeling as if were his fault that she was a widow and betrayed. Perhaps her marriage would assuage his lingering guilt.

'But she is indispensable with my children,' John said, gazing after the two women. 'I cannot spare her.'

Both women were widows, of course, but he had spoken of only one of them. 'I was speaking of the Lady Valerie.'

The words seem to break the man's trance. 'Ah, yes. I've asked her to join the Queen's household for a time.'

Gil frowned. He wanted to see no more of this woman. He wanted to be rid of her and the reminder of his failures.

'Besides,' Lancaster continued, 'she seemed less than eager at the thought of a new husband.'

For some reason, that irritated Gil, too. Surely it was not because she mourned the first one?. 'What does she think to do? Go to a nunnery?' Perhaps it was the wimple that made him think of that. He had the sudden urge to rip it off and see her hair flow free. What colour would it be? Looking into her dark eyes, he had not even noticed the brows above them.

'She seemed to want to tend to her rye crop,' the Duke said, with an amused smile.

Gil shook his head and shared his lord's smile. Well, she was in no position to refuse a new husband, even if he treated her no better than the last one. She would marry the man Lancaster chose and it would be none of his concern.

The war, however, was. 'The invasion, Your Grace.' The title due a king still strange on his tongue. 'Men and ships should be ready by summer. I recommend we land in Portugal and march into Castile from there.'

An attack from an allied country instead of a direct assault would ease their way, avoiding a battle until the men and horses had landed and were ready to fight. Gil had been a strong advocate for Portugal. If Lancaster chose his plan, surely he would also name Gil to lead the men.

'Pembroke argues for Navarre,' Lancaster said. 'And others for Galicia.'

'Portugal's King sees the pretender as an immediate threat. He should be willing to support us.'

'Until we hear from the ambassador, we cannot be certain,' Lancaster said. He leaned closer and dropped his voice to a whisper. 'And my father the King has plans as well.'

'To return to France?' Vast swathes of the country once firmly in their grasp were splintered and they were on the brink of losing the land that had spawned a line of kings three hundred years old.

He nodded. 'But speak of it to no one now.'

Gil nodded, but held his tongue. The last time he had seen the King, who had once been the greatest warrior in Christendom, the man had seemed tired and weak. But if he was now well enough to conduct a campaign...

Well, Castile, not France, was Gil's responsibility. 'For our own campaign, then, I will proceed.' Money, men, ships to move them must be ready before summer, the season for war. 'Plymouth is the port best positioned, so I will direct the ships to gather there and—'

'*Mi Señor y Rey.* A word.'

The Castilian priest, with no more respect than to interrupt his 'King' at conversation.

Gil waited for the Duke to dismiss him.

That was not what happened. 'Yes, Gutierrez, what is it?'

'You should issue a proclamation immediately to announce that you have assumed the

title of King. A statement that will challenge
the man who pretends to the throne. I can, of
course, draft such a document, but I require
an office from which I can assist you and La
Reina in conducting affairs of state.'

'Ask my steward to find you proper quarters and whatever assistance you need to do
so.' All Lancaster's attention was on the trappings of kingship again, as if it were a relief
to deal with a fanciful kingdom instead of a
real war. 'I'll sign and issue it as soon as it
is ready.'

'And to do that, Monseigneur, we must create a seal. The arms of Castile, combined with
your own leopards and lilies, perhaps.'

A genuine smile. One of the few Gil had
seen from the Duke all day. 'Yes. I like that.'

Documents. Signatures. Seals. The country would be taken by men, not by proclama-
tions. Yet here was Lancaster, chattering with
this Castilian about the design of a royal seal.

'Your Grace?' Gil called. 'The invasion
plan?'

A wave of the hand, but the man did not
turn. 'Tomorrow, yes.'

He watched Lancaster and the Castilian
walk away, and when they paused for the
Duke to present the priest to Lady Kather-

ine, Lady Valerie stepped away, standing beyond their circle.

Yet she was the one who drew Gil's gaze. Surrounded by the colour and noise and bustle of the hall, in her plain garb and wimple, she was still, calm, almost frozen, like one of the statues of the Virgin Mary.

Thinking of her lost husband? Or of the woman who had last loved him?

The dirty silk burned like an ember against his chest.

Abruptly, he left the Hall and walked outside. The winter air would clear his head.

The sun was low in the sky and daylight fading fast. Looking out over the darkening river, he tried to remember more of Lady Valerie's husband. Gil had been a commander who prided himself on knowing his men, yet he had noticed nothing unusual about Scargill. Men in war satisfied their needs as they must.

He wondered who the woman had been. Not a noble woman, he was certain. Not a lady deserving of a knight's devotion. One of the camp followers, probably. He could barely tell one from another except for the laundress who did his washing. But in the midst of war, strange things could move a man's passions.

Faced daily with death, a man might cling to a woman as a way to cling to life…

And a man's wife never to know better.

The frigid air blunted the smell from the river and when he reached the edge of the quay, he pulled the dead man's token from his tunic, as soiled and stained as the relationship itself. He held it over the water, then dropped it into the darkness. For a moment, the white fabric drifted like a feather. Then it hit the river and was sucked beneath the waves.

His duty was done. Never to be thought of again.

He turned back to enter the palace, feeling a moment's sympathy for Lady Valerie. Better the Duke marry her quickly to a man who would get some children on her and make her forget.

He hoped her new husband would be kinder than her last.

Chapter Three

Valerie joined the Queen's household in the Savoy Palace but as the days went on, she saw little of Constanza, or La Reina, as the Queen liked to be called. Lent had begun and the woman spent most of her days either on her knees in her chapel or on her back in her bed.

Of Castile's 'King', Valerie saw nothing at all. Lancaster settled a generous sum on his wife, so the Queen could run her household as befitted her rank.

And then started coming the gifts.

Week upon week, the Clerk of the Wardrobe would arrive at the door with another treasure for the Queen of Castile and deliver it into Valerie's careful hands. Cloth of gold. Circlets set with emeralds and rubies. Loose pearls by the handfuls. Pearls enough to fill buckets. Pearls to be made into buttons, sewed on dresses, sprinkled on adornments for her hair.

Wealth such as Valerie had never imagined, placed in her care. And she would take each offering to the Queen, telling her it was another gift, a mark of respect from her husband. And each time, the woman turned her head away, muttering.

'El único regalo que quiero es Castilla.'

Valerie had learned enough words by now to know her meaning.

The only gift I want is Castile.

Her faint connection to Castile had touched the Queen, but it had no such effect on the ladies surrounding her, who were less than pleased to have another *Inglésa* added to the household. Not only did the Castilian women not speak the language, they had no interest in learning anything of England and, as a result, Valerie heard neither news nor rumour from the court.

She and Lady Katherine, both ignored, clung to each other's company. The Queen's ladies did not invite them to gather for music or needlework and if the English ladies entered the room, the Castilians hovered close to the Queen as if to protect her from danger.

'Do they think I plan to steal her child?'

Katherine muttered one evening as they sat together in their rooms by the fire. 'I have my own children to mind.'

Valerie flinched. Perhaps the Castilians had seen the hunger in her own eyes, for it became evident, as February's days grew longer, that the Queen was with child. Shapeless gowns and cloaks had masked her condition when she arrived, but in the privacy of her quarters, it was plain to see.

And Valerie, whose womb had never held a babe, was seized by sinful envy.

God had made both Constanza and Katherine fruitful. Where were the children of *her* womb? Had God forsaken her? Or would things be different with another man?

'The Queen and her ladies are alone in a strange country,' she said. She would feel the same, she was certain, if she were ever exiled and sent to an alien land. 'I'm sure that is the source of their fear. Not us.'

'I have seen little fear in that woman,' Katherine muttered.

Valerie could not disagree. When La Reina did rise from her bed, she was straight-spined and clear-eyed and the orders she issued about the ceremonies of her exiled court showed that she had no doubt of her title and position, here or in Castile.

'But her ladies all seem angry,' Valerie said. Despite all her smiles and attempts to appease them, there had been nary a nod in return. 'What if she complains to the Duke of our care?'

Katherine smiled, serene. 'Do not worry. He knows.'

As if he knew Katherine so deeply that... Not a thought to be followed. 'You served his first wife. He knows your worth. He knows nothing of me.'

Katherine laid light fingers on her arm. 'I will not let that woman undermine you.'

Perhaps, Valerie thought. But this Castilian court in exile was all that stood between her and a new husband. If the Queen decided to be rid of her, there would be no recourse.

A knock on the door. A page entered. 'The Queen commands your presence, Lady Valerie.'

She rose, uncertain whether to rejoice or be afraid.

'Here. Let me.' Katherine tucked a stray hair back beneath her wimple. 'Now you look lovely. Go. See what the woman wants.'

Valerie followed the page to the Queen's quarters.

Constanza, La Reina, sat in a throne-like chair, wearing a headpiece unlike any Valerie had seen in the English court. It hugged her head, with beading draped around, and came to an upward point in the middle of the forehead. It hid her hair, but made her eyes look huge.

Her priest, who served as her interpreter, was at her side.

Valerie curtsied and stood, waiting. Whispers.

'You are a widow,' the man said, finally.

She touched the wimple. '*Sí*, Your Grace. My husband died in the service of your husband.'

More whispers, then the priest spoke again. 'La Reina still mourns her father. She understands your pain.'

Valerie bowed her head and murmured her thanks, while sending a silent prayer that the Queen would never, truly, understand how she felt about her husband's death.

A silence, then. Awkward.

The Queen was struggling to hold herself erect, though it was evident that carrying the heir was not easy for her. Valerie had heard her complaints ranged from bleeding in her gums to rawness of the throat and stomach. And, now, in the same room with her, Valerie could smell that someone had broken wind.

'I have not properly congratulated Your Grace,' she said, hurriedly. 'That you are to become a mother.'

The Queen smiled, an expression more joyful than Valerie had ever seen from her. No, it was beyond joy. Near heavenly bliss.

The priest translated her words. 'Yes, praise God. When we return to Castile, it will be with a son. My father will be avenged.'

'Dormit in pace,' Valerie muttered, with bowed head. The Castilian King had been murdered by his half-brother, who now held the throne that should have gone to Constanza.

Suddenly, the Queen touched Valerie's head and gave quick instructions to the priest who spoke again. 'La Reina will have a hundred masses said for the soul of your husband.'

'A hundred?' Valerie had paid the four pence for her husband's death mass and, truth to tell, she wondered whether the sum could have been better used paying a labourer to repair the roof of the barn.

Quickly, she prayed to be forgiven for

such a wicked thought. The man would need prayers if he were to move beyond Purgatory to rest in peace, though she suspected he would find many kindred souls there, waiting for purification before they could go to Heaven.

She dipped in reverence and bowed her head again. 'Her Grace's generosity is beyond measure.' For one hundred masses, she could have bought a horse and chariot. 'If there is any service I can render her, I will gladly do so.'

A smile touched the woman's lips, even before the translation was complete. Perhaps she knew more of the language than she admitted. Or, more likely, the posture of deference and gratitude was the same in her country as here.

Murmurs, and then the translator spoke. 'You have been patient to stay here. You must want to go home. She asks only that you continue to pray for victory in Castile. Rise. Go with God.'

A dismissal.

And the word home.

She fought the swift desire to see her Kentish soil again. If only she could, truly, go home. Instead, she would be forced to submit to a new husband, an unknown terror, one who might be even worse than the last.

But if the Queen had sensed her desire for home, she would have to convince her that she wanted nothing more than to continue in her service. 'Your Grace, I had hoped to serve you, at least until the child is born.' Spoken in haste. When was the child due?

The translator frowned. 'La Reina has many ladies.'

'Yet none but Lady Katherine and myself know the court and the language.'

Constanza flinched as if she had just tasted a bitter fruit. *'Me gusta. Esta mejor,'* she said, looking directly at Valerie.

This one, better. She meant Valerie.

Ah. So there *was* something about Katherine the Queen did not like. Perhaps she feared Katherine's loyalty lay more with Lancaster than with her. Whatever the reason, deference to the Queen's wants might help her meet her own.

She touched her ancestor's brooch. A reminder. 'As you know, Your Grace, I carry the blood of Castile.' Or, so she had been told. In truth, after a hundred years and multiple generations, the amount of Castilian blood she carried would run out if she pricked her finger. 'I would be honoured to serve La Reina as she unites again the two great nations of Castile and England.'

She waited, silent, as the words were translated. A frown, a furrowed brow would mean she was held in no more favour than Lady Katherine.

The Queen studied her. Valerie kept her eyes wide and a hopeful smile on her lips.

Finally, the Queen nodded, then muttered a few words.

'*Hasta unas semanas*,' the priest said. 'Until Easter. And then, we will see.'

Only a few weeks. Well, she was grateful for even a brief reprieve. 'I will strive to serve Your Grace in all things.'

And the things most important to Constanza now were her child and her country. Well, those things would now become important to Valerie.

It was either that, or it would be some nameless husband who would decide what was important and what was not. At least Valerie could understand the longing for a child. And for home.

She bowed her thanks and left, wondering again who Lancaster would choose to be her husband, when, for some reason, Sir Gil's face flashed across her memory, full of shock when he discovered Scargill had been false and he realised that the scrap of silk was not hers. The stern look in his light blue eyes had turned into one she might almost have called compassion.

Surprising, that a seasoned man of war would expect such virtue from one of his men. More surprising that he might think that she would expect it from a husband.

Because for all the protestations of chivalry, marriage was an exchange, with no more passion than the purchase of flour in the marketplace. It was true for the Queen of Castile, and true for Valerie of Florham.

She knew that, even if Sir Gilbert Wolford did not.

Not until March, when Lancaster sent Gil to summon the Lady Katherine from the Queen's quarters, did he give himself permission to think of Lady Valerie again.

He had rarely seen her over the past few weeks. The palace was large, the Queen's retinue kept to themselves and he was more interested in finding ships to carry the men across the Channel than in the Scargill widow.

And yet, she had lingered in his thoughts.

Had the Duke selected her new husband? He found himself hoping Lancaster would choose a nobler man than Scargill.

Although he had come to the Queen's quarters to summon the Lady Katherine, it was Valerie who caught his attention when he entered the chambers. She was sitting quietly in a corner of the room, still swathed in the black of mourning, with her eyes downcast. There was something small and neat and held back about her, as if she was trying not to take up too much space.

'Ladies.' He bowed, hoping Valerie would raise her eyes. 'My Lord of Spain asks the Lady Katherine to come to him with word of his children.'

Lady Katherine smiled when he said it, bright as sunlight. 'Of course.' She rose and hurried from the room, not waiting for him to escort her, leaving him alone with Lady Valerie.

And silence.

He should have left as well. There was no reason to stay. But her stubborn refusal to look at him seemed a challenge. Had someone told her of his past? Or was she still blaming him for her husband's death?

The chatter and whistle of a black-and-white bird, caged in a sunny corner of the room, shattered the stillness.

She lifted her head, abruptly, and when her eyes met his, he glimpsed again how much she hid, though he could not say what it was. Anger? Fear?

She stood, abruptly, and tried to brush past him to reach the door.

'Wait.' His hand on her arm again.

She looked down at his hold, as if uncertain whether it was an assault or a caress, and when she lifted her gaze to his again, she had shielded all emotion. 'Why? Do you bring a command for me, as well?'

Anger, then. At him.

He let go of her arm. What had possessed him to grab her like that? It was as if his family's blood could never be truly conquered, despite all his years of struggle.

He stepped back. 'Your husband's spouse breach...it was not my doing.' And yet, he felt responsible.

She shrugged. 'It is the way of all men, all marriages.'

'No. Not all. Lancaster's marriage to the Lady Blanche...' He let the sentence fade. The Duke's devotion to his first wife was the stuff of legend. Fodder for Chaucer's verse.

'So I have been told.' A sigh, then. 'But this marriage...' She shrugged.

Yes, the Duke had a new wife now. One to whom he did not seem so devoted.

And then, a gasp. She touched her fingers to her lips, as if to take the words back. 'I did not mean to suggest that My Lord of Spain, that he...' She looked beyond him, in the direction that Lady Katherine had gone, and then met his eyes.

Wordlessly, they asked each other the same question. Was it... Could it be...? Had Lady Katherine been summoned because...?

'No, of course not,' he said. An idea not to be thought. Not to be suggested.

Neither looked away, now. Neither spoke. And before he could stop his thoughts, a spark leapt between them. His breath came faster, his pulse beat more quickly. He was lost, now, in her wide-open, brown eyes. No longer was he thinking of what the Duke might do, but of himself and Valerie, together—

She blinked, then backed away and circled the room, as if trying to escape what had just passed between them. 'I only meant,' she said, not looking his way, 'that His Grace has been busy and we have not seen him here in the Queen's quarters.'

He, too, tried to fill the air with denials, both spoken and silent. 'And the Queen has not emerged from her rooms.'

'Because she is with child,' Valerie answered, still pacing. The magpie flapped its wings and began to chatter, as if to join the conversation. 'It is difficult for her.'

'Yes, that is true.' Gil nodded, surprised that his tongue could still form words. 'He knows she needs rest.'

Now that Valerie was safely beyond his reach and no longer gazing into his eyes, he could think clearly. The bird's chirp filled the quiet air, sounding too much like laughter. Gil's unwanted surge of desire ebbed, replaced by a safer emotion: resentment. How could she suggest that his lord behaved as anything less than the epitome of chivalry? 'He has sent her gifts,' he protested. 'Jewellery.'

At the word, Valerie's steps halted. The bird fell silent, as if waiting for her to speak. Safely on the other side of the room, she finally raised her head and met his eyes again. 'Do you think,' she said, her words now soft, but deliberate, 'that La Reina cares for pearls and gold?'

Remembering the disdain with which the Queen had set aside the gold cup presented to her, he suspected she did not. 'What *does* she want?'

'To go home.' Her gaze turned towards the window, as if she, too, was drawn to that place. 'Home.'

Home. Castile.

'Lancaster wants the same.' Of that, he could assure her. 'As do I. We are gathering men and horses and ships, developing a plan to return.'

'When?' A simple word. A challenge.

The same one he had flung at the Duke. Instead of a decision, still they waited for the ambassadors to Portugal, and now, for the cardinals meeting with the Valois King.

'War is not so simple.' He spoke harshly, his own frustration sharp on his tongue. Simple on the field, yes, where a man must kill or be killed, but to get that far—well, that was straining his patience. The Duke had still made no commitment to a plan. Or to a leader.

'Nor has it been simple for La Reina, yet she has done all he asked. She has wed him, given him her claim to the throne. Now, she carries an heir. When will he fulfil his vow to her?' Spoken with as much passion as if she were the one wronged.

Easier, perhaps, for her to argue for what

the Queen wanted, instead of her own desires. He understood that. He shared the sharp disappointment of the expedition's delay, but he could not criticise his lord for what could not be controlled. 'It takes time.'

Meaningless words for all he dare not say. King Edward, too, needed men and horses and ships to go to France. The Duke had the means to mount his own invasion, but still, Parliament would have its say...

Valerie raised her eyes heavenwards and shook her head. 'Yet war is what you do. It is your life. Do not tell me you and Monseigneur d'Espagne do not know how it must be done.'

It *was* his life, his path to redemption. And yet, she spoke as if he were the greenest squire.

'You state your judgements plainly, Lady Valerie.' Was this the same woman who had lowered her eyes, afraid to speak? Here again was the warrior he had glimpsed when they first met. 'You will find that no one is more diligent in duty than I. And no one, not even My Lord of Spain, is more dedicated to the cause of Castile.'

Suddenly, she became again a timid mouse with downcast eyes, biting her lip and looking down at the worn oak boards of the floor as if she were a servant who had spoken above her station. 'Forgive me. It is not my place to say such things.'

'Not unless you have commanded men in war.' Yet he found himself as irritated by her sudden humility as by her criticism. Which was the real woman? 'You know nothing of Castile.'

She lifted her head. 'Little enough. But I have wondered about it. Always. What is it like?' Neither anger nor fear in her voice, now. Only curiosity.

What is it like?

Five years past, and still, Castile was stamped on his soul. But when he thought of it, he thought not of the march over the snow-covered mountains, nor of the victory in springtime's battle, nor even of Lancaster's praise of him as a man 'who cared not two cherries for death'.

He thought of the King's Palace of Alcázar.

Queen Constanza's father had not lived in a cramped, dark castle. Not for him a building constructed with blocks of cold stone, designed only to repulse the enemy in battle. Instead, the stone of Alcázar was carved into patterns as delicate as lattice work. The rooms opened into courtyards that dissolved into rooms again, until there seemed no difference between inside and out. Beneath a hot, bright blue sky, Gil had stood, surrounded by the sound of splashing fountains, calming even when you could not see them. Wherever he looked, every floor, wall and even ceiling was covered with designs that served no purpose other than to delight the eye. Red, white, blue, yellow—patterns so intricate his eye became dizzy trying to follow them.

There was nothing familiar. No reminder of home or England. And no secrets buried in the earth.

There was only peace. Peace he had thought never to find.

Peace he longed to feel again.

But what man noticed fountains or remarked on coloured tiles? It was the conquest that he should summon for her. The things *El Lobo* would remember.

For he had been sent to that place, to that palace, to collect the payment Castile's King had promised. It never came. Finally, instead, the King handed his two daughters to the English to settle the debt.

He wondered whether Constanza had told Valerie that part of the tale. 'It was freezing. Then boiling. And then the Prince fell ill.'

The Prince, Lancaster's brother, heir to the English throne, had been felled by the flux. Near three years later, he had not recovered. Many wondered whether he ever would.

She blinked at his blunt words. 'I had thought it a gentler land.'

'Is that what the Queen tells you?' No doubt the woman remembered home through the eyes of a child.

No doubt the Queen longed for Alcázar as well.

Valerie shook her head. 'That was the story passed down through my family. That it was a country of warm sunshine and cloudless skies.'

'Your family?' Had he misunderstood? 'I did not know you were Castilian.'

She shook her head. 'Not really, but when Eleanor of Castile came to marry the first Edward, she brought her ladies with her, just as Constanza has done. Many of them married English knights, my ancestor among them. Her memories have floated down to me.' Her gaze, distant, as if she could truly see a land she had never known.

Memories. As changeable as sunlight flickering on a stream. Except for the ones too strong and stubborn and dangerous to disappear.

'Then you must long to see it in fact,' he said. Perhaps they shared that desire.

She tilted her head, looking as if she had never thought of it before. 'Until My Lord of Spain reclaims the throne, it matters not whether I would or no.'

Her words, no matter how gently spoken, seemed thrown like a gauntlet to challenge him.

It was true. All his longing meant nothing until English soldiers sailed for the Continent. Until then, his yearning to return to the solace of Alcázar was no more than a promise. 'All of us who serve the Monseigneur d'Espagne know our duty. To him, to his Queen and to his heir. We will attain Castile. And hold it.'

No. It was more than a promise. It was a vow.

Chapter Four

When next he was summoned to Lancaster's quarters, Gil again saw a warrior all energy and attention.

Now, today, finally. I will be chosen to lead the army of invasion.

For some reason, his first thought was to share the news with the Lady Valerie.

In fact, so certain was he that the time had come, he almost did not understand the words Lancaster actually spoke.

'We need more ships—' the Duke began.

'More?' The last time he had assessed the situation, they had ships and men in hand and were only awaiting word from the ambassadors about their route. 'Why? Have the Portuguese refused an alliance?' If so, they would need more ships for a frontal assault.

'Not for Castile. My father the King is

sending Pembroke to relieve the siege in France.'

King Edward, Lancaster's father, was King of this island. His will came before all. Uneasy, Gil counted again the men pledged to war. 'Do you intend to divert our men to his effort?'

'No.' A promise as unequivocal as Gil would have wanted. 'Pembroke will take a small group with him and gold to recruit the rest when he lands in Brittany. From there, they will march through Aquitaine...'

Gil listened to the plans by habit, each word bitter in his ears. France had belonged to the Plantagenets before England. They could not let it be taken now.

'We await word from Portugal,' Lancaster concluded. 'So it will not delay our own expedition.'

Portugal's silence, other forays diverting ships and energy—Gil was losing patience with all of it. But a commander must know when to advance and when to hold back. When they did reach Castile, his weeks of frustration would all be forgotten.

'I will leave for Losford tomorrow,' he said. Losford, guardian of the English coast, was the castle where he had learned to be a knight, all those years ago. In the harbour below, there must be some shipowners who would be glad of some extra coin to ferry men and horses across the Channel. For this effort, cogs, even smaller boats could be pressed into service. 'I'll send men to Sandwich and New Romney, too, and—'

A hand on his shoulder. 'But something else, first.'

Again, his hope swelled. 'Anything.' At last. *Captain of the Knights of Castile...*

'You must marry.'

'What?' He shook his head. He must have misheard. They had talked of war, not weddings.

But Lancaster's words were firm. 'Marry. You must marry.'

'Of course, my lord.' How could the man think of marriage when Castile lay in the balance? 'Some day.'

'Now.'

'My lord—' he began. Had the man gone mad? 'Now is not the time—'

'It must be now. Before...' He let the word drift.

Before he took up arms again. Before death threatened.

'My lord, marriage can wait.'

Lancaster shook his head. 'You have waited longer than most men. You want a wife, do you not?'

He had never pondered it as a question. Marriage was not a choice. Every man married. But for him, marriage had been a long-deferred dream, not to be undertaken until his own accomplishments shone so brightly that they would make people forget the shadows that clung to the Brewen name of his mother's people.

When he thought of it at all, he vaguely imagined a time when he was revered and honoured and living in Castile, where one day, he would look out and see a special glance, a special woman, one who could be as dear to him as the Duke's first wife had been to him.

A foolish dream. But he was certain that when he was the man he wanted to be, the woman he wanted at his side would appear.

'Yes, Your Grace, I do. When the time is right.'

'And children? You want children?'

He wanted a son. Wanted with the same fierce longing that a starving man yearned for bread. 'When we hold Castile, my lord.' When he could return to the gardens of Alcázar, this time, as one who belonged there. 'Then, gladly.'

The Duke shook his head. 'You cannot wait. If anything happens to me, the Queen will bear my heir to sit on the throne. If we lose my brother, his son will sit on my father's throne. If something happens to you...'

If something happens...

Death could come today. Tomorrow. By accident or disease. In France as easily as in Castile.

Lancaster had sired four sons. Only one still lived. He was a man who knew the shortness of life. Gil knew it, too, but he somehow believed he could hold death at bay until he had redeemed the Brewen name.

The Duke cleared his throat. 'The leader I choose should think of the future.'

Was marriage, then, a condition of his appointment?

Gil swallowed. 'Who?' he said, finally, testing the thought. 'Who would you have me marry?'

He had never actually devised the image of a wife. A son, with eyes the same pale blue as his own, he had imagined in detail so precise the boy might as well be real. But the woman who would warm his bed and wake up beside

him day after day for all the years to come?
He had not envisioned her at all.

Valerie's face flashed before him. Why
should he think of her now?

'I have chosen,' his lord said, 'the Lady
Valerie.'

Gil fought the quickening of his pulse. Had
the man plucked her image from his mind?

But she was nothing he wanted in a wife.
She shared his passion for Castile, perhaps, but
from the words they had exchanged, he did not
think they would suit. Stubborn, opinionated...
He had thought to marry someone...different.
Someone who would not remind him of his
failures. 'But we are in the midst of a war. The
King wants ships. There is no time—'

'There is time enough to bed her.' A grim
smile from the man who had bedded his wife
somewhere between France and the English
coast.

Now Gil's blood swirled hot and his body
surged in response, as if suddenly given permission. To know the colour of her hair, the
feel of the skin of her shoulder beneath his
fingers—that tempted him beyond reason.
'But my duties to you, to Castile...'

Lancaster waved his hand. 'None of that

will change.' And then, a wisp of memory
clouded his face. 'Mine didn't. Not this time.'

But Gil wanted, needed, change. If he married now, he would have no home to offer but
the one he had fled. 'But surely this marriage
can wait until we regain Castile?'

'I said things would not change,' Lancaster
said, 'but changes will come, Gil, as they do
to all men, whether you want them or not.'
Memories and regret, both stamped on the
Duke's face. 'Which is why your marriage
must be now.' The words, final. Allowing no
more debate.

He swallowed. 'Is she…willing?'

The Duke looked baffled. 'She is a woman.
She will do as I bid.'

And so must Gil. In truth, the decision belonged neither fully to him nor to her. True,
either of them could protest at the church door,
but the church ruled life *after* death. Lancaster, Monseigneur d'Espagne, ruled their
lives on earth, hers as well as his. Their relationship with their lord was a complex series
of agreements and promises, many written on
parchment, others written on the heart, but all
bonds made of honour, strong as iron. Vows
not to be broken.

Not if Gil was to be the man he wanted to be.

But his true question lay answered. *Will she have me? Will she take a Brewen?*

He asked a different way. 'Her family…will they consent?'

'She has no family left. And no children from Scargill, so none to compete with the ones you will give her.'

He nodded, silent, understanding why the Duke had thought her a good match. No family left. No one to object.

'She told me,' Gil began, 'that one of her ancestors had served Eleanor of Castile.'

'Yes,' the Duke said. 'Her family has no stain through all those generations.'

He gritted his teeth. An awkward acknowledgement. He needed a spotless reputation from a wife more than he needed worldly wealth.

Assuming his agreement, the Duke continued. 'Her dowry is the parcel of land given to the family years ago, but it is part of Scargill's holdings now and he died with debts. I will arrange a dowry payment for her instead of passing on the land.'

Because a duke could do such things.

'Does she know? Of your decision?'

The Duke smiled. 'I thought you should bring her the good news.'

He wondered whether she would find it so. 'I leave for Losford tomorrow. When I get back—'

'No. Now. Before you go.'

He sighed. Maybe fortune would smile on him, he thought, as he bowed and left the room. Maybe, as opinionated as she was, she would say no.

'Sir Gilbert asks that you come to him.'

Valerie looked around the room. The page's whisper had reached only her ear. The Queen was resting and her other ladies, as always, were ignoring Valerie with deliberate purpose.

She would not be missed.

She put down her hated needlework and followed the boy to the outer room, struggling to stifle the heat in her cheeks at the memory of their last meeting. Her every encounter with Sir Gilbert had been unpleasant. What could send him to her again? Did he think to warn her against spreading suspicious tales about Lady Katherine and My Lord of Spain? No need. Idle chatter would only hurt both Katherine and the Queen.

The grim set of his lips did not reassure her. The Wolf of Castile they had called him. He looked the part today. Whatever message he bore, the tidings must not be good.

What was that legend?

If a wolf sees a man before the man sees the wolf, the man will lose his voice. If the man sees the wolf first, the wolf can no longer be fierce.

Then surely he must have seen her first.

She stopped before him and he bowed, briefly. 'I must speak to you alone. Let us walk.'

She gave the page a wave of dismissal and followed Sir Gilbert into the corridor. His stride was longer than hers and she near ran, trying to keep up, but still she lagged behind.

He turned to look finally, still frowning.

She stopped, still a length behind him, and mirrored his glare. 'My steps are shorter than yours.'

A flicker crossed his face, as if her words had shamed him.

Again, she had been forward, speaking as if she had the right to counter him. Would he shout? Raise his hand to her? No. He did not have a husband's rights. She was safe.

He waved towards a window alcove with a stone seat. 'Then sit.'

She did. The hallway, far from the nearest fireplace, was empty and the stone was cold even through the wool of her gown.

He did not sit, but towered over her, broad shoulders blocking the draught from the window, looking more fearsome than ever. She braved meeting his eyes again, but this time, she sensed none of the fire that had sparked between them before.

This time, he eyed her as if she were an opponent on the field.

She wanted to avert her gaze—to study the cloud-filled sky and assess when the rain would come—to look anywhere but into his critical eyes. But she willed herself to face him, calmly, waiting.

He began without preamble. 'The Duke thinks I ought to marry you.' Words spare, blunt. And totally void of feeling.

Yet they left her as shocked as if he had run a sword through her. All hope for a life of independence, even the few weeks' reprieve she had tried to grasp, all gone. She clawed for words. 'But I am serving the Queen.' As if that might truly save her. 'She asked that I stay—'

'You will continue to do so as long as she wishes.'

Only until Easter, La Reina had said. And there could be no wedding until Lent was over. But then? She would indeed be at a man's mercy again.

She paused, letting her mind settle. She must not assume the worst. They were gathering men and ships to return to Castile. This man had other obligations and no time to settle into a new household. 'So we will be betrothed. For some time.'

'No.' His face was grim, as if he took no more joy in this marriage than she did. 'Before I sail for Castile.'

And yet, she had heard nothing of when that might be. Did she have weeks? Days? Only hours of freedom left? 'When? When is this marriage to take place?'

How many more days of her own did she have?

'A few weeks. The war is close upon us.'

Obvious the man had not married before. He knew nothing of all that lay ahead. 'But banns must be read, the union announced—'

'Lancaster will see to that.'

'I see.' And now she did. No arguments to be made. No way to delay. The decision had been made. Once again, control had left her hands and been given to men. She fixed a smile on her lips, met his eyes with the appropriate expression and mumbled the words he must have expected from the first. 'I am honoured, of course, and will try in every way to please you.'

The compliment brought a moment of confusion to his face, a touch of doubt to his gaze. 'Does that mean yes? That you will marry me?'

She wanted to scream *no* to this man she barely knew. Was he cruel or kind? Had he wealth or only his armour?

And yet, all that mattered less now than what *he* knew.

He *knew* of her humiliation. He knew that her husband had betrayed her with another woman. Seen the crumpled evidence of her failure as a wife.

Suddenly, knowing she would have to please a husband again, the familiar fears returned. Would he, like Scargill, think her breasts too small and her hips too thin? Would he, too, grow to hate the sound of her voice and tell her to shut her mouth?

And even though she must expect that this man, too, would seek another's bed some day, the first time he came to *her* bed, he would already count her a failure. He already knew she had not been enough for her husband.

And yet, he had asked. *Does that mean yes?* An awkward question, but surprisingly kind. As if pretending the choice were hers. It was not. For she had known one thing, always. No woman could refuse a marriage.

And so, with head high and lips pressed firmly into a smile, she nodded. 'Yes. I will marry you.'

I will marry you. Words enough to satisfy canon law. That would allow her to call him husband.

He let out a breath, as if with her assent, the hardest part had passed. 'Then we are betrothed.' Yet that look of uncertainty lingered on his face, as if the Wolf had become a Lamb. 'Have you nothing more to say?'

She coughed, to cover the laughter that threatened to bubble over. A woman did not laugh at her husband. Not if she wished a smooth existence. But this man seemed full of contradictions, by turn stern, angry, kind and even, for a moment, as uncertain of the future as she.

There were questions she should ask, important ones about her land and his family, where they would marry, where they would live. But the answers barely mattered now. My Lord of Spain had decreed it. So it would be. All she could do was to bow her head, bite her tongue and submit to this man's will. 'What happens next?'

'I have duties with my lord, as do you with the Queen. We will continue to fulfil them.'

She nodded, as briefly as he, with a half-smile as if his answer pleased her. It was a partial, but perplexing reprieve. 'But I am to meet your family, move my belongings, settle into your holdings and establish a home...' When she had married Scargill, there was a flurry of activity, settling details of property and management of the holdings, making room for him in the home that had been hers...

All to be ready for the arrival of a baby that never came.

'Nothing will change.' He said those words as if they were a vow, then rose, as if the conversation was complete and everything settled.

Nothing? It was evident that the man had never married, or he would know that *everything* was to change. Or, perhaps, it was true for him. Only Valerie would, once again, rearrange her life to accommodate a husband. And, if he had no home of his own, perhaps they would live at Florham, as she and Scargill had done. The very possibility was a comfort.

'Is it my place to tell the Queen that I am to be wed?' How were such things done? Her life had been tied to the earth, not to the court.

He shrugged. 'Perhaps it is for My Lord of Spain to do. I do not know the way of such things.'

'As you will, my lord.'

He shrugged his shoulders, as if to throw off the title. 'You must not call me that.'

My lord. It was the title Scargill preferred above all others. 'But so you shall be.'

'Call me something else.'

'The Wolf?' She permitted herself half of a smile. 'I think I prefer my lord.'

'My father called me Gil.'

'Gil.' A name bright and strong. Easy to speak. 'Then it will be as you wish. Gil.'

He nodded, awkward, then stood. 'Tomorrow I go to Losford on behalf of the King. We will discuss arrangements when I return.' Duty done, he bowed. Brief. Perfunctory. 'Goodnight, Lady Valerie.'

His task complete, as if dusting his hands of dirt.

He was three steps away when she called after him. 'If you are to be Gil, I must be Valerie.'

He looked back, then honoured her with a stiff nod, as if every interaction was painful.

But then, he took a step towards her and did not look away. Tangled in his gaze, she rose from the bench and moved in his direction. Time slowed. Her pulse quickened. Close now, she could see his lips, no longer unyielding but softer than she had thought. One breath more, two, and they would make another step, touch, and—

'Goodnight, Valerie.'

And then, he was gone.

Nothing will change.

She only wished it were true.

Chapter Five

After he told the Scargill widow he would marry her, he vowed to think of her no more.

He did not succeed.

For the two days it took to ride to Losford, he thought of little else.

He had faced few battles for which he felt less prepared. With sword and shield, he was at home. No man would ever call him coward. All the lessons of honourable men at war were now his own, ready to pass on to his son.

But the courtly manners, the ways to woo and the honour due a noble woman, those had been harder to conquer. He had delayed the study of them, thinking them unimportant. So now, when the moment came and he was forced to ask a woman to be his wife, he had not known what to say.

Yes, she had agreed, though he would not

have blamed her if she had wanted a different match. *If I am to meet your family*, she had said, as if she had no hesitation and knew nothing of his past. Was she really ignorant of his history? If so, what would happen when she discovered…?

Too late to wonder. She had agreed. The matter was settled. He would marry and have the son he had always wanted.

And the legacy he wanted for the child? Castile twinkled before him like a distant star. When he needed solace, he would think again of the colourful courtyards, far from the forests of Leicester. There, in the sun, well away from his home where the Brewen name meant only disgrace, his son could grow to manhood with pride.

As Losford Castle's crenellated corners came into view, looming over the narrow band of water between England and Calais, he was reassured. This place was more home to him than his own.

Here, he had taken his first steps towards redemption.

As a lonely boy carrying a disgraced name, he had served as page and then squire to the Earl, one of the most powerful men in England. Before he was felled on the field in

France, the man had moulded Gil's character and his skills.

There had been no time to send a messenger, but the guards recognised his colours and before he had dismounted, Lady Cecily, the daughter of the late Earl, and her husband rushed into the courtyard and embraced him.

'It has been too long,' she said, in the chiding, loving tone a sister might use.

Her husband, Marc, let a clap on the shoulder speak for him. They shared the quick smile of fighting men.

It had been eight years since Marc had taken pity on him after the Earl died and had taught him new ways to hold his shield and swing his blade.

In those days, it seemed England had vanquished all her enemies. As a new knight, still green, Gil feared he might never have another chance to prove his worth in battle. A false fear. There had been chances aplenty. That he had survived was a testament to Marc as well as to the Earl.

They hustled him into the warmth of the castle and settled before a fire, the stone walls blunting the howl of the wind. A cup of wine. The smell of roasting lamb. The faces of friends. He took it all in, let the weariness of the ride, and the years, and the urgency of war flow away, and basked in the welcome peace.

What would it be like, to have a haven like this? Would the brittle widow ever smile to see him as Cecily did when she looked at Marc?

But these two had defied a king for their love, not been ordered to the church door as near strangers.

'It is so good to see you.' Cecily's voice, bringing him back to the room. 'I keep hoping to hear word you're to wed.' She raised her eyebrows, expectant.

He cleared his throat. Now, he must speak. 'Only this week,' he said, 'the Duke has chosen a wife for me.' A word still strange on his tongue.

'Who? Tell me!' There was delight in her voice.

'I know little of her.' Suddenly, the thought of all he *would* know rushed through him. The scent of her skin. The feel of her lips. Whether she slept at night on her side or on her back. Not things he could speak of. 'She is the widow of one of my men.'

Cecily laughed. 'Well, perhaps you might tell us her name.'

'Valerie.' It was not the first time he had

spoken it, but this time, he realised how many times he would say it from now on. The word, the woman, both attached to him into eternity. 'Lady Valerie, widow of Scargill.' The man's name, distasteful now.

'Lady Valerie of Florham?' She sounded pleased. 'Her family has lived for generations some two days' ride from here.'

'Do you know her?' Eager, suddenly, to find a connection between his bride and Cecily, who had been like a sister to him.

She shook her head. 'We have never met, though I know of the land and the family.'

Her family has no stain. 'An honourable family, Lancaster said.'

'Truly.' Cecily and Marc exchanged glances as if they did not need words to understand one another and, for a moment, Gil was jealous. He wanted that kind of love, the kind that needed no words. 'How does she feel about…?' *About marrying a Brewen.* 'Your family?'

'She did not say.' Again, the questions plagued him. Did the Duke select her because she could not protest? Or was she simply ignorant of misdeeds of long ago and far from her own corner of the island? If the latter, he should tell her. And then, she might say no, he might be free—

He sat straight. His own disappointments, petty, not worthy of mention. 'That is not why I have come.'

He put down the wine. The moment for peace and comfort had passed. 'Lancaster prepares to sail for Castile and the King gathers ships to send an expedition back to France.'

Marc's expression hardened. So quickly, he, too, became a warrior again, ready to fight.

And Cecily? Not for her the fearful face so many women donned at the mention of war. Only a brief glimpse of sadness, soon gone. 'Does King Edward not command his men?'

Cecily had been too long away from court. She could not know how much the King's strength had failed and how often he was absent from the Hall.

'I am certain Lancaster is consulting His Grace and his brother on every decision.' Said too quickly. Said as if England's greatest warriors were still leading the fight. He sighed. They deserved to know the whole of it. 'But the truth is, neither the King nor his oldest son is a well man.' An admission hard to make.

For more than forty years, an Edward had led English men to victory. What would they do now?

Did Cecily and Marc exchange a glance? What secret message did they share now?

But she had grown up in this castle, inherited it and held it for England. It was the bulwark that served to stop anyone who dared cross the Channel. 'Losford is ready,' she said. 'What does the King need?'

'Ships. Cogs. Anything that floats on water.'

'Not men?' It was Marc who spoke. He had come to England as a French hostage and stayed for love, promising to defend King Edward's shores. But would he be willing to invade his own country?

He put a hand on Marc's shoulder. 'No. We do not ask that of you.'

A brief moment of relief. And then they spoke of other things: how many vessels were ready now, how quickly the rest could be raised. Clear, now, that the expedition would not sail on the King's schedule.

'You have my thanks,' Gil said, finally. 'As well as those of My Lord of Spain.'

'Who?'

So caught up in the doings at court, it had not occurred to him that Parliament's decrees would not be quickly known throughout the island. 'The Duke of Lancaster has taken the title, now that he has married the rightful heir to the Castilian throne.'

Marc's expression said clearly how foolish a title that seemed.

A young boy dashed into the room, slowing his steps when he saw a stranger. 'Denys,' Marc said, 'this is Sir Gilbert Wolford.'

Immediately, the boy squared his shoulders, tamed his smile and bent his head in greeting.

Cecily smiled with a mother's pride. 'Our son, Denys.' She put a hand on the boy's head and ruffled his hair. 'Who is awake beyond his time to sleep.'

The boy—was he seven? Eight?—had his mother's dark hair and the shape of her face, his jaw even more square than hers, coupled with the light brown eyes of his father.

'Sir Gilbert,' she said to him, 'was fostered by my father.'

Gil smiled, trying to put the boy at ease. 'Your belsire was a good man and a great warrior.'

'The boy must leave us this year,' Cecily said, her tone wistful.

Leave to be fostered. Just as Gil had done

when he came to be taught by Cecily's father. 'Who will be his teacher?'

'We have not yet decided.'

The years of his training unrolled before him in an instant. As a page in this very castle, he had learned to serve at table, recite poetry and care for the battle steeds. Then, as a squire, he learned to wield first a wooden, then a steel sword and to keep the lord's armour ready until he, himself, was knighted. 'Would you consider me? I could teach him all his grandfather taught me.'

There was silence as the two exchanged looks again. But they did not say yes.

He rued asking. Every time he thought he had earned the right, he faced a reminder. This child was heir to one of the greatest titles in England. And even Cecily's fondness for him was not enough to allow her to give her child into his care.

'An idle idea,' he said, quickly, as if he had spoken without intent. 'I am about to go to war again.' Boys no older than this one would accompany their knights, not into battle, but in the path of harm, even so. 'The boy is too young for that.' An excuse, but it would serve.

'I am not!'

'*Chut*, Denys,' his father said.

'Your father is right, Denys,' he said. And something hurt in his heart as he saw this proud, stubborn young boy. No, a Brewen would not be good enough, but some day, a mighty lord of Castile might be. 'Before you train for war, there are years of learning manners and poetry.'

The boy's face said clearly what he thought of that. 'It is fighting and honour I must learn, not poetry.'

Cecily pulled her son to her, a gesture both chiding and protective. 'I would keep him with us a little longer.' The words of a mother, not a countess.

Denys squirmed, trying to shrug off her embrace. 'I want to go now! With Sir Gilbert.'

Gil looked at the boy, the son he did not yet have, as eager for war and glory as Gil himself had been when he knew no better than to be fearless. He exchanged a glance with Marc, then leaned towards young Denys. 'Once you leave here, you will seldom see your home or your parents again. Take another few months. Your parents will find the right man to entrust with your training.' He clasped the small shoulder. 'Be ready.'

The light brown eyes lit up. The nod and the smile were firm and steady. Yes, this boy would make as good a warrior as his father and grandfather.

Cecily stood and took the boy's hand to lead him to bed. 'Besides, we cannot ask Sir Gilbert's promise before he has the chance to speak to the woman who will be his wife. To her will fall the burden of his first training.'

Only at her words did Gil realise he had never thought of consulting Valerie about this decision.

He mumbled something, suddenly understanding, despite his confident statement, how many things in his life were about to change.

After Sir Gil spoke to her of marriage, Valerie whispered not a word of the conversation to anyone.

She heard nothing from her husband-to-be, who had travelled to Losford. Nor did the Duke reach out to confirm the news and, as the days went on, she wondered whether she had heard aright.

'He says we are to be married soon,' she complained to the magpie, one day when they were alone in the room together. 'And then he disappears for days without a word!'

The bird tilted his black head and made a series of sounds, with the up-and-down lilt of a sentence, which clearly sounded to Valerie like, *You poor dear. Isn't he a problem?*

'Yes!' And then she smiled, unsure whether she was amused at the bird or at herself for fancying he answered her.

Perhaps the proposal had been an illusion. Perhaps, if she remained silent, the world would stay as it was and when Easter came, she might be able to go home.

But after a week of uncertainty, she could stay silent no longer. Alone with Lady Katherine one afternoon, she spoke the words aloud. 'My Lord of Spain has chosen Sir Gilbert Wolford to be my husband.'

Husband.

She waited, silent, uncertain whether she hoped Lady Katherine would confirm what she had said or dismiss the idea.

She got a soft smile and a quick hug. 'I wish you both well.'

Real, then. She would be the man's wife. The feel of his hand, warm on her arm, floated into memory. She swallowed. 'Thank you.' Easier to say than she had feared.

'What did John tell you of Sir Gilbert?'

John. She had called the King… *John.*

I did not mean to suggest that My Lord of Spain…

Valerie flushed with the memory. Meeting Gil's eyes, denying any accusation about Lancaster's conduct, and all the while, fighting the flutter in her own heart at the knight's nearness.

What if it was true? What if Katherine and the King…?

She could not ask, of course, but she must be alert and search for signs. Better to know the truth and keep a prudent tongue.

'My Lord of Spain has not spoken to me. It was Sir Gilbert, Gil, who told me the news. And he said so little…' She thought back on all he had refused to say and shook her head. 'What can you tell me of him?'

Katherine shrugged and dropped her hands from Valerie's shoulders. 'I know little of the man.' She looked away.

'But I know even less,' Valerie said. His reputation was fierce, Lancaster trusted him, but had he something to hide? If Katherine was so close to the King, surely she would know. 'Is he…demanding?'

A gentler word than *cruel*, for if he were, who would tell her so?

A brief look of surprise. 'I know my lord holds him in high regard.'

'As he did Sir Hugh?'

A frozen stillness touched Katherine's face. She had said nothing of her husband to Valerie. 'I am certain he did, yes.'

Silent, Valerie, too, averted her eyes, afraid she had somehow seen something too…intimate.

But then, a rustle, a clearing of the throat, and Katherine spoke again. 'Sir Gil is a capable warrior and a trusted adviser. I am certain my lord thought he would be a good match for you.'

And yet, Katherine looked as if there were more unsaid.

'They called him The Wolf of Castile.' Valerie shivered.

'A compliment to his prowess. He is a fearsome warrior.'

Fearsome to the enemy. Would he be so to her?

'Valerie?'

Gil's voice sounded behind her, breaking her thoughts. As if speaking of him had summoned the man. And yet, now that she knew he was there, she seemed to sense him with her whole being.

She lifted her head, turned and caught her breath.

He was taller than she remembered, but his

face was just as stern, as if he disapproved of
her. No, worse. As if he disliked being forced
to rest his eyes on her. There had been moments, when they had looked at each other,
when she thought, perhaps…

Had she been wrong? Was her life to be
lived with a man who disdained to look on
her? Perhaps he would be willing to come to
her only in the dark, only when he could bed
her without seeing her—

'I must see to the children,' Katherine said,
quietly slipping out of the room to leave them
alone.

The door closed behind her, leaving the
chatter of the caged magpie to fill the silence.

Valerie fixed her smile in place. A small
smile, a bowed head, these had appeased
Scargill. For a time. 'I am glad that you had
a safe journey, my lord.'

His frown, reminding her.

'I mean, Gil.'

This time, he nodded, though without a
smile. 'And you? Have you been well?'

A slight hesitation in his words, as if he
might, in truth, care that she had been well.

She nodded. Did the man, indeed, have
compassion? If he, too, wished to avoid this
marriage, perhaps they could—

'Lancaster obtained a special licence from the Archbishop...' he began, all hesitation gone. 'We can wed any time after Easter.'

Words so cold, so devoid of all feeling that she felt as if he were discussing how to load a boat.

She knew better than to look for passion in a marriage. Every time her mother had been widowed, she had selected a new husband with the same assessment she would bring to the picking of the ripest apple from the tree. And yet...

'My family is gone...' she began. The father who had died before she was born. The mother who had wed two more husbands. Only the land remained. The land that had been given to them by the first Castilian Queen. 'So we will wed on your holdings in...' She waited for him to speak.

'Leicestershire.'

To the north. Far from Kent. A place she knew nothing of. 'We will wed in Leicestershire, then.'

'The special licence allows us to marry anywhere, not just in our home parish. The ceremony will be held here, with the court.'

'So your family will come here. Your parents—'

'Died long ago. No one will come.'

'Why?' A question too sharply asked. Was he ashamed to have his people meet her?

He shrugged, his face like stone. 'There is no one you need meet.'

No one had spoken of his family. Even Katherine had sidestepped her questions.

Smile. Look accommodating. 'Then after we are wed, we will go there. You will show me the land, I will meet—'

'No.' He broke his gaze and walked to the window. 'I have not visited in years.'

'But your serfs, your crops, those must be managed.'

'A steward handles those things.'

His response remained firm and calm while Valerie felt her grip on her temper weaken. 'He must do an excellent job, if you do not need to oversee his work.' She could not keep the edge from her voice. In her experience, stewards needed guidance. Careful guidance.

'That is not a life I like.'

Not a life I like. As if he could choose.

'Then where are we to live?' The words slipped out before she could stop them. Sharp, insistent, demanding.

He looked surprised. 'In Castile, of course, where My Lord of Spain is King.'

Castile. Said in the same tone of reverence the Queen used, as if the strange, foreign soil were the Holy Land. 'I believe,' she said, between gritted teeth, 'that a king currently resides there.'

He stood taller and took a step, as if he had been attacked, but he did not raise a hand. 'That King usurped the crown. Until Castile is ours again, we need no home but the court.'

'I see,' she said. She did not. How long would living be postponed while they searched for this Holy Grail? Yet no disloyal doubts could be spoken before the Queen. It seemed this would be true with her husband, as well. So quickly she had forgotten her wifely duty...

She bowed her head. 'I will do whatever you ask of me,' she said, in a voice more calm than her mind.

'I shall ask nothing of you.'

His voice like a hard, cold wind. She raised her eyes to see a face just as harsh.

The few things her first husband had asked of her, to join his body, had not been pleasant, but they had been her duty. If this man asked nothing, what would her purpose be? What would she do? 'Nothing?'

A shift on his face. As if she had caught

him in a lie. He spoke again. 'Nothing but a son.'

Now, she turned to ice. He asked for the one thing she was not sure she could give.

'You know,' she said, 'that I have no children?'

He nodded, showing no surprise. 'Then it is time.'

Oh, yes. Time and more.

Now she was the silent one. She had done whatever her first husband asked of her, but she had failed in her most important duty. Certainly, it was not for lack of effort on his part. She closed her eyes against the memories of their bed, where she would lie beneath him, gritting her teeth against the pain, waiting for it to be over...

Was she barren? She did not know. Even her mother had not borne a son, despite taking the seed of three different husbands.

I must stop fighting. I must not question. Just do as he asks.

'Assuredly,' she murmured, then remembered to curve her lips upward. 'A wedding wherever and whenever you like.'

'It will have to wait,' he said, in a voice empty of desire. 'Until we secure ships for the expedition to La Rochelle.'

'But I thought, I mean…' Cloistered with the Queen, Valerie had paid little attention to the preparations for war. She knew little of the world beyond Kent, but even she knew that La Rochelle was far from Castile. 'I thought you sailed to return La Reina to the throne.'

He shook his head. 'That must wait. There is a siege in Thouars. King Edward sends a force to relieve them.'

Eyes wide with shock, she opened a mouth full of questions…

And he was gone.

Chapter Six

After Gil was safely out of earshot, Valerie let fly a word she had heard Scargill utter in his angriest moments.

Thankfully, there was no one to hear her except the black-and-white pie bird, who squawked with appropriate horror.

She began to pace again, trying to walk off the anger she had worked so hard to hide.

'We are to marry, but he refuses to tell me anything about his family or his home.' The bird chattered back, as if he understood. 'He speaks of nothing but Castile and then says we are not going there.'

She paused with a sigh and stopped before the cage. That reprieve, at least, was a blessing. She longed for Florham, where every inch was well loved and familiar. 'What, Sir Pie Bird, am I to do?'

The bird puffed out his white body and chattered an answer, though this time she could recognise neither English nor Castilian words. Ah, well. At least he was a creature she could address without fear.

The bird had been a gift to La Reina, but Constanza had developed an aversion to the black-and-white creature with his blue wings and green tail feathers, saying he was not like the birds of her home. But to Valerie, he was exactly like the pie birds in her garden, stealing morsels from the kitchen and picking insects off the rose bushes. She had moved the cage into the room she shared with Katherine and kept the poor thing fed.

'I wish, I wish...'

She let the sentence die.

Her mother had named her Valerie, after a saint who was beheaded when she refused to marry a pagan. The saint had risen from her grave, carrying her separated head, so the story went, and, if that were not miracle enough, made a gift of it to the bishop who had converted her.

Valerie's mother claimed she chose the name as a reminder to stay strong in the midst of adversity. Valerie took a different lesson from the tale: never refuse an offered marriage.

Certainly, her mother had been forced to wed quickly when Valerie's father died and left his pregnant wife a widow. And yet another husband followed after that one, too, died. Her mother seemed to expect nothing of either man except that they keep mother and child fed, clothed and at Florham.

So Valerie knew she could expect nothing more. And yet…

'So what would you tell me, Sir Pie Bird? How can I accept my lot?'

And the bird, in some combination of whistles and croaks, made a sound very much like, *Dios te bendiga, mi hija.*

Bless you, my daughter.

How many times had she heard the priest murmur that to the Queen? The bird, it seemed, had picked up the foreign words. How was it that a bird could learn Castilian and yet the Castilians could not bother to learn her language?

And yet, her husband did not intend for them to live in England, it was clear. She, too, would be living in isolation in a strange land whose language she did not know, just as the Queen was. No wonder the woman had tried to recreate Castile within the small corner of the Savoy she controlled. When Valerie was stranded in Spain, she might want to do the same.

She felt an unexpected connection with La Reina. They were both women who might be forced by marriage to live in a foreign land. And did the Queen know any more of what was to come than Valerie?

Lancaster had not bothered to tell his wife of Valerie's marriage, she was certain. Well, no matter how these things were done, she was going to take the news to La Reina herself, for it seemed that their fates were even more connected than she had thought.

'I wanted to tell you myself, Your Majesty,' Valerie began, when ushered into La Reina's presence the next day, 'that I am to be married.'

'Married? *Casarse?*' The Queen had not waited for the translation to be complete.

A deeper curtsy. Had she angered the woman? 'Yes, Your Grace. My Lord of Spain has chosen Sir Gilbert Wolford to be my husband.'

A whispered conference between the Queen and the priest, establishing which English knight she meant. Then, the priest turned to her again.

'La Reina wishes you well in your marriage. When is it to take place?'

'I am not certain,' she began, 'but he has said soon, because of the invasion.'

As the translation was made, the Queen smiled, nodding. *'El ejército naviga por Castilla.'*

Castilla. Said with the confidence of expectation.

Valerie licked her lips and glanced at the priest. Did the Queen know less than she?

It was not her place to speak to the Queen of military matters, but she deserved to know. At least, Valerie thought she did.

'And to France, as well. Sir Gilbert gathers more ships so men can sail to La Rochelle.'

The Queen blinked and turned to the priest. *'Qué quiere decir La Rochelle?'*

The priest frowned. He was the liaison to the Queen's husband. Had he known that men were being sent to France? If so, he apparently had not bothered the Queen with the unpleasant news.

Another whispered conference and a puzzled look from the Queen. Had the priest translated her faithfully?

'This man,' the priest said. 'The Queen asks, does he care for you?'

No. He had not conveyed what she said at all. Someone did not want the Queen to know of the war plans. Her husband?

Even a queen, it seemed, could not force her husband to reveal everything.

'Yes, Your Grace.' Of course he would care for her. That was the purpose of marriage. 'He is also a loyal servant to you and to My Lord of Spain and will work without ceasing until we regain Castile.'

A small smile from the Queen. She must have understood a few of the words: servant, My Lord of Spain, regain Castile.

'La Reina is pleased,' the priest said, as if her expression had needed translation.

Valerie smiled in return. 'Easter will be soon upon us and La Reina had said I might stay until then. That means I will soon be taking my leave.'

If the Queen dismissed her and Gil refused to take her to Leicestershire, perhaps she could go home, at least for a few weeks. She might be there in time to witness the buds form on the quince tree and if the warmth came early, to see the white blossoms blushing with the soft pink of a sunrise—

'No, that will not be necessary. La Reina

will be glad to have you in her household as long as your husband allows.'

Valerie froze, silent. Trapped. Even the Queen did not ask of her desires, only of what her husband might want. And her husband did not understand, none of them did, that she wanted nothing more than to return to the earth her ancestors had held since the first Edward sat on the throne.

She blinked, hoping they had not seen her shock. *'Gracias,'* she murmured, followed by the expected words. *As you wish. Honoured to serve you.*

It did not matter what she said. The priest would turn her words into whatever he liked.

But as Valerie left the room, it was with a new vow. It was time for her to conquer the foreign tongue. Today, she served the Queen. Some day, she might be exiled to Castile. Either way, she needed to know more than *gracias*.

The priest and the pie bird must not be the only ones in the household to understand both English and Spanish.

In the coming days, she tried Castilian words whenever she could, but none of the Queen's ladies would help her understand their language. They tittered at her accent when she tried and mispoke, yet they did nothing to help her say the words correctly.

One afternoon, they all gathered to listen to minstrels, sent by Lancaster to entertain them. The music needed no language to be enjoyed, but still, while she and Katherine smiled, the Queen's ladies remained expressionless.

Finally, as the performance ended, Valerie tried again.

'*Me pareció que la música era mara-villosa. La disfruto?*' The accent sounded wrong, even to her ears, but certainly they would understand she complimented the performance and asked whether they had enjoyed the music.

The Queen's sister Isabel giggled, but no one spoke, either to correct or to answer her.

Then, the pie bird chirped in answer and repeated what she had said in better Castilian than hers.

The ladies looked at each other, at the bird and at Valerie.

She swallowed, afraid to speak. Would they think she had tried to teach the bird? Would they think her disrespectful? Would they even think she had sent the bird to spy on them?

And then, an unfamiliar laugh, as if rusty with misuse, filled the room.

The Queen was laughing.

As if given permission, the others joined in. Valerie let herself smile.

A flurry of conversation between the Queen and her translator, who spoke to Valerie. 'La Reina says we cannot have the bird speaking better Castilian than you.'

'Maravillosa,' the Queen said, with a smile, correcting the pronunciation. *'Sí, fue maravillosa.'*

Valerie repeated, carefully, hoping the lilt was correct, and was rewarded with applause from the other ladies.

It was a step.

She hoped Gil would be pleased.

Later, Gil thought of all the things he should have said to his future bride. He should have smiled, flattered her, turned the talk to pleasantries. Instead, when she had asked of his family, all he had done was fling up a wall, as if to blunt an attack.

Did she expect him to repeat all the tales she had no doubt heard? That, he would not do. And yet, he had been neither courteous nor kind. He was to marry the woman. He must, at least, learn to be pleasant in her company.

Next time, he vowed, things would be different.

Yet he did not see her again until the days leading up to Easter. Even the reclusive Queen of Castile attended the celebrations on Maundy Thursday, when all gathered in Westminster Abbey to witness King Edward dispense alms and wash the feet of sixty selected 'poor'.

The men whose feet the King was to wash, stood in an obedient line, looking more awkward than honoured.

Gil sympathised.

Years ago, Edward had decreed that on this occasion, he would wash the feet of one beggar for every year of his life. Now that he had reached his sixtieth year, the line seemed endless, even to the restless crowd watching. As the hours dragged on, far from standing in quiet and solemn witness, the court began to mingle, chattering in whispers.

Constanza's ladies stood close to Lancaster's men. Gil looked for Valerie, smiled when she met his glance, but she only nodded and looked away.

She did not move to join him.

Instead, the Lady Katherine came to his side. 'I understand,' Lady Katherine began, 'that you and the Lady Valerie are to wed.'

'So My Lord of Spain has commanded,' he said, wondering whether Lancaster or Valerie had told her. Gil had shared the news with no one at court.

'You sound as if the choice does not please you.'

He paused. He did not know enough of the woman to be pleased or displeased, but marriage now, to any woman, was a distraction, an obstacle. 'Of course I am grateful for my lord's interest. If I seem displeased, it is only because I think the wedding could wait until we regain Castile.'

Not entirely the truth, but all he would say.

'There it is again, your stern look.'

He shrugged. 'It is my face.' As a boy, he had trained himself to don a fierce expression, protection against all the hurtful words so that no one could ever know when a cruel taunt had hit its mark. 'I cannot change it.'

Nor did he want to.

'It has made her fear you.'

His cheeks burned. He called it anger at Valerie for gossiping to this woman. It was not. It was shame. He turned to look at Lady Katherine. 'It is my family she fears, I vow.'

A shake of the head. 'She does not know.'

'Are you certain?' Yet, increasingly, it seemed she did not. That would explain her willingness to have him as a husband. 'I thought all the world knew.'

'Her home is far from yours. The stories are old.'

Old, perhaps. To some. 'I still hear them whispered, even here.' He looked over the crowd. Always, there seemed to be someone looking at him with disdain. Always, there were those who would not speak to him at all. 'Surely someone at court has told her.'

'She has spent little time with anyone else except the Castilian ladies.'

Those women, at least, had never heard the Brewen name. Perhaps she had, indeed, been sheltered from the gossip of the court.

'But she has spent time with you.' The two women had obviously exchanged confidences. 'You did not tell her?'

Lady Katherine shook her head. 'I did not think it my place.'

And it was not. It was his own painful confession to make.

The Lady Katherine was looking at him, as

if waiting for his promise, and he found himself wishing that someone else would tell her,
sparing him the need.

'We have had little time for courtship,' he
said, unsure whether he was trying to make
excuses to Lady Katherine or to himself. 'And
this...' he cast his eyes around the arched,
holy space '...this is not the place.'

He had vowed to be more pleasant to the
lady. Telling her his family history would be
unpleasant indeed.

'But she will discover the truth in time.'
Katherine turned to meet his eyes.

She would. He knew that. And yet, he
wished for a wild moment that they could escape to Castile, escape his past as he had always wanted, and that she might never know.

What kind of marriage could they have
then? The kind he had always longed for?

He shook his head. 'I know. Just not...
today.'

'Bad beginnings can ruin even the most
promising of marriages.' She put a hand on
his arm. 'And I want to see her happy in her
marriage.'

'Most are not.' Refusing to voice his own,
dimming, hopes.

Her silence seemed to stretch long. 'I know,' she said, finally.

And with those words, she left his side.

One thing was now clear. He had thought Valerie feared him because of his blood. Apparently, the truth was worse. She was frightened by him, even not knowing who he was.

All her questions, all her probing, he had taken as her attempt to make him tell all. Instead, she had only wanted the most basic facts that a wife would need to know.

Bad beginnings. Yes, he and Valerie had had a bad beginning and, when she discovered the truth, it would only get worse.

Now, he saw Lady Katherine nudge Valerie in his direction. She came towards him, slowly, eyes downcast, the very picture of fear, finally throwing a glance back at Katherine when she had reached his side.

Trapped. Well, despite Lady Katherine's manoeuvring, he would not speak of his family today.

He cleared his throat. 'Have you enjoyed the ceremony?'

Valerie gave him a sideways glance. 'More so than the King, I suspect.'

He assessed the line. 'Only five more.'

She smiled. 'He seems to be getting faster as he nears the end.'

The ceremony had begun as a careful ritual. The King had dipped each man's feet into the basin, first the left, then the right. Then, with a clean cloth, he had dried each one, taking care to wipe between the toes. Finally, he had placed alms and bread into each beggar's waiting hands.

'I think,' Gil said, with a grin and a wink, 'I saw damp footprints as the last man walked away.'

She doubled over, trying to stifle an inappropriate laugh, managing to turn it into a coughing fit before it could disrupt the decorum of the day.

He felt quite pleased.

The King finished the last dirty foot and was helped to rise. The priest blessed the congregation and the court filed towards the door.

'Who is the lady?' Valerie asked. 'The one beside the King.'

'She is the King's...' He looked around. Did one say aloud the King's mistress?

The woman was so young she might have been his daughter. She hovered close at hand now, always, displacing the royal attendants, so that, it seemed, the King need only think of a thing and she made it appear.

'She is...close to His Grace.' He could not keep the tinge of judgement from his voice. Certainly it was too much to expect a man to be faithful to a wife after her death, and yet... 'Her name is Alice Perrers.'

'Ah, I see.' Valerie nodded, without a trace of hesitation, surprise or disapproval, and looked over her shoulder, for a final glimpse. 'I understand My Lord of Spain thinks her good for the King.'

He never seemed to know the way of a woman's mind. Particularly this woman's.

Still, King Edward looked better than the last time he had appeared in public. Gil wondered whether credit could go to his mistress, brazen enough now that she appeared at his side, even on a religious occasion.

The court spilled out of the Abbey and into the sunshine. Queen Constanza was helped into a litter. Lancaster chose to ride a horse, but most walked. Gil fell into step beside Valerie, though it was a struggle to shorten his stride. He wanted again to make her laugh, but pressured to be merry, he could summon only serious thoughts.

Easter was early this year. It was still

March and a sharp wind cut the air. Two ladies of the court hurried by and he caught a few words before they were snatched away.

'...cares for Lancaster's children...service of Venus, too.'

'I saw her leave his quarters...'

The two walked ahead. The rest was lost.

Was that how it was?

He glanced at Valerie, but she seemed to have heard nothing.

He was not a man to listen to court tattle, but even he had wondered... And if it was true, had the Duke himself suggested Lady Katherine remind him of his duty to his wife?

Or, perhaps, it was no more than a rumour.

A high-pitched laugh shattered the air, too loud to ignore. He looked ahead at the flock of Castilian ladies, unable to tell one from the other.

'The Queen's sister,' Valerie said. 'Isabel.'

He had been presented, he was certain, but he could not remember her. 'She seems most unlike her sister.'

'They are of very different natures. Isabel enjoys the company of others, even if they are *Inglés*. If she does not understand what is said, she simply laughs.'

The path curved with the river and the wind

whipped from behind them. Valerie hunched her shoulders and he put his arm around her.

Close, now, he realised anew how small she was. He could tuck her under his arm, envelop her in his cloak, even pick her up and carry her and not strain with the effort. But walking beside her, trying to match her steps—that was a challenge.

'By next Easter,' he said, as they reached the Savoy stairs and started to climb, 'we will be in Seville. And it will be warm.'

She did not answer quickly. 'I was told they celebrate differently there.'

The Easter he had been in Castile had been spent on the march, not in church. 'In what way?' They were all Christians. He had never wondered that the ceremonies might differ.

'It seems,' she said, so softly that he had to stoop to hear her, 'that men walk through the city, whipping themselves, as a way to share the pain of Christ's suffering.'

'Really?' This must be symbolic, as a way of teaching. 'As we might watch a mystery play, you mean.'

'No. They use a scourge. With nails.'

'But the church has banned the Flagellants.'

'Yes, but it permits devotees to pay tribute to the suffering of Christ during this week of his death.' Her dark eyes, wide with horror, met his now. 'They told me the streets run red with blood.'

He shuddered.

Life was full of pain aplenty. Why would any man seek more?

But the very thought stopped him from further talk and he murmured a brief farewell when they reached the palace.

Perhaps, he thought, as Valerie disappeared, the Queen's ladies were simply exaggerating. But if not, this was a Castile far different from the peaceful garden he held in memory.

Which one was real?

Chapter Seven

Summoned to Lancaster's quarters just after Easter, Gilbert was prepared with a report. The King had first decreed they would sail for France on the first of May, only a month away, impossible, as even the King now knew. Despite all his efforts, there were not enough ships in England to launch battle on two fronts.

But he had found enough ships to carry a small force, enough men to defend against pirates and enough gold to hire troops once they made land in Brittany. That would leave the bulk of the fleet to carry men and horses to Castile, under Gil's command if all went according to plan.

But when he entered, Lancaster spoke first. 'There is news,' the Duke said. 'The French and the Castilian pretender have joined forces. And fleets.'

For a moment, Gil was not certain he had heard aright. 'A combined fleet?' They had known, of course, that France's ruler supported the Castilian pretender. But they had expected combined armies on land, not a defence of the Continental coast. 'We do not have enough ships for battle before we reach the shore...' he began. Not unless they abandoned plans for Castile.

'Their plan is not to engage at sea. It is to invade England.'

Unimaginable. The Channel had protected the island nearly as effectively as a moat. 'Are you sure?'

News from the Continent came late and changed with each messenger. Poitou was under siege. French ships would land in Wales. Could any of it be believed?

'We cannot take the risk.'

Gil nodded. If it were the French alone, he would not worry. Over the years, the French had tried scattered raids on the English coast with little success. But Castile had ships and men to rival England's. If Castilian ships were ready to sail, England might be facing an enemy landing on its own shores.

And so again, a new plan. He started to assess.

'Losford will hold,' Gil began, 'but we must send them word.'

'And set up watch points to scan the sea,' the Duke added. 'And light the fire, to spread word if they come.'

'We can divert some of the ships to patrol the coast. I will leave at once—'

'No. The celebration is tonight.'

In the midst of preparations for war, Lancaster had decreed that a pageant be held to celebrate the end of Lent and the heritage of the Kingdom they had not yet won. Queen Constanza and her giddy sister Isabel had dictated some of the food and entertainment, he had been told, in an attempt to bring Castile's culture to the halls of the Savoy. 'But if our shores are threatened, it should be cancelled.'

'No. The Queen must not be told.'

'What?'

'Nothing must disturb her. Or the child she carries. I made it clear to her translator. She must hear only good news. And tonight, we rejoice.'

Rejoicing was the last thing on Gil's mind as he stood in the Hall that night. It was a celebration, yes. Even Lancaster's father, King Edward had come, a sign of his support of his son's ambition to be a king in his own right. His appearance was like a blessing that conjured past glories and past triumphs, seeming to assure future success.

No wonder Lancaster wanted nothing to spoil the evening.

But as Gil approached Lancaster, who was in an intense conversation with the man who would command the expedition to France, it was clear that smiles were only on the surface.

'Surely My Lord the King of Spain cannot plan to give command of the Castilian invasion to Wolford. He's a...' Pembroke looked up as Gil approached and fell silent.

But the way he looked at Gil said it all: *You cannot give such a command to a Brewen.*

The past suddenly came alive again. The jeers of the squires who had shunned him. The doubtful looks when he first rode to battle. The ladies who had looked the other way when he smiled at them.

If he had hoped Valerie would not discover the truth, he hoped in vain. The old stories, the old pains, would never die.

'What were you going to say?' Gil asked, belligerent, daring the man to hurl the insults to his face instead of whispering the stories behind his back.

A moment's hesitation. Pembroke bit his lip. Not so brave now. 'My lord and I were only discussing the invasion plan.'

'Enough,' Lancaster said, putting an arm on Gil's shoulder. 'Do not question my judgement, Pembroke. Sir Gilbert has fought by my side with bravery and honour. I will hear no ill spoken of him.'

The man nodded, silent, and backed away. No, Pembroke would not question Lancaster again, but he would remain convinced that Sir Gil Wolford was an outlaw instead of a knight.

'He does not speak for me,' Lancaster assured him, after Pembroke took his leave. 'I have no doubts.'

Grateful, Gil murmured thanks as Lancaster was drawn into another conversation. No doubts, he said, but also, he had not yet named Gil his commander.

Sometimes, it seemed that My Lord of Spain was the only man in England who did not doubt him. Enough reason for Gil to give the man unwavering loyalty.

And a reminder that Castile remained his goal. On the Iberian plains, they did not know the Brewens. They knew only *El Lobo, un hombre de honor*, a label he was proud to wear.

He looked for Valerie, finding her, finally, across the Hall, somehow in the centre of a discussion between the Queen's ladies and the court musicians.

'What is Valerie doing?' Willing to brave a question to Lady Katherine, hoping she would not ask him if he had told Valerie the truth. 'There, with the women and the minstrels?'

'I believe she is trying to help them explain how Castilian dance music should be played.'

'How would she know that?'

'She has made a great effort and learned a few words of Castilian. And, a task even more difficult, she has taught the Queen's ladies some words of our tongue.'

He looked again at the woman who was to be his wife—small, dark-eyed, her expressions hard to read. Did he know anything of her? How could a woman so meek as to fear his glance mediate among the cacophony of agitated voices in two languages? Finally, he glimpsed again the woman he had first met— strong and unafraid to speak her mind.

But if she was trying to learn the language, it was a sure sign she shared his devotion to Castile and to the marriage, despite all. He al-

lowed himself a smile and a moment of pride.
A wife who knew the language would be an
asset indeed.

In the midst of struggling to imagine
a translation for *animado*, Valerie looked
around the Hall for Gil.

Despite the spirit of celebration, he looked
as stern and angry as ever as he spoke to the
Duke and another nobleman. Only when
Katherine joined him did Valerie see a fleet-
ing smile cross his face.

It was when he looked at her.

She smiled in return. Could she have
pleased him in some way? How?

But she had little time to ponder it. Queen
Constanza had left her chambers to go somewhere besides church and the 'court in exile'
had developed a special entertainment of Castilian song and dance. The Castilian ladies
had forced every page and squire at their dis-
posal to masquerade as if for a disguising.
Their faces had been smeared with cinders
and their clothes decorated with ribbons and
bells, as gay as Yuletide jesters.

Valerie's few Castilian phrases had been
pressed into service, though how successfully,
she feared to discover.

The musicians were given their final instructions, with a waving of hands, then Valerie stepped away, fingers clasped as if to pray, and the dance began.

Gil joined her at the side of the dais as the men began to hop about the floor. The music and the rhythms were as foreign as the language she struggled to learn and she had no idea whether the result was what they had hoped. She could only pray that La Reina would be pleased.

The crowd at the edge of the floor pressed in on either side. Gently, Gil moved her in front of him, so that no one would stand before her and block her view.

She struggled to keep her mind on the dance. She knew Gil was a strong man, but she had not been so close to him for so long before. Short as she was, no taller than his shoulder, he could easily see over her. Close and strong at her back, she felt his hands on her arms, steady, sure.

When Scargill had put his hands on her, he meant to cage, force, trap her. But Gil's touch spoke of protection, as if he wanted to make certain she was not shoved aside by a careless courtier.

Surrounded by his strength, she felt safe.

And hopeful. Perhaps he would be a kinder husband than her last.

She turned back to the dance.

Foreign movements. Strange looks. She did not know if the result was truly Castilian or only a poor translation, as awkward and uncertain as her words had been.

And when it was finished, the men on the floor stood, struggling to smile, looking at each other.

Silence reigned in the Hall.

Then, the self-styled King of Castile stood and clapped, long and loudly, until, finally, the rest of the room joined him. Sitting beside her King, La Reina beamed with joy, as if for the first time since she arrived, she felt at home.

Valerie's eyes met hers and she was rewarded with a nod. Some joy, then, in giving the woman a taste of all she had missed.

More familiar music filled the air again, and Gil's hands fell away as the audience became a crowd once more.

'It was supposed to be a dance of Castile,' she said, wincing as she looked at him. 'Did you see anything like that when you were there?'

Gil gifted her with another smile. 'I believe they do it somewhat differently in Spain.'

She laughed. 'I would not be surprised.' Still, both the Queen and Gil seemed pleased. 'I do not understand why their faces must be darkened.'

'There are Moors in Spain. I think this dance is one of theirs.'

A reminder of all that awaited her. Her smile faded. 'Is this is a heathen dance?' She would not have thought the devout Queen would want to see such a thing.

'It is not so unusual there. They are superb horsemen and they can create places of great beauty.' The thought seemed to take him away. 'You will see. When we are there.'

An unwelcome reminder.

Castile loomed like a dragon over her. Nothing would be familiar. Not the land, the weather, or the language. And now, to discover it was peopled with strange, dark beings...

'Lady Katherine said you have learned some Castilian,' he said, his tone warm with approval.

Was that was the reason he had smiled? 'I have tried. The Queen and her ladies speak nothing else. I could not help but learn a few words. But then they wanted me to explain a Castilian dance I have never seen...' She looked to Heaven. 'I was not at all certain that my meagre interpretation was helpful.'

And yet, this brief triumph, this moment in which she had made both the Queen and Gil smile, this had been because she had tried something new, as strange and foreign as it had been.

'You have done well to master even a few words. I learned little more than three phrases during all the months I was there. We were ever in search of a translator.'

A translator like the priest, who she was certain, had filtered her words to the Queen. What else had he kept from the woman? Had she any knowledge of what was happening around her?

'Then how could you be sure the translation was right? That your meaning had been accurately conveyed?' In diplomacy and war, what could be more important than understanding what friends, or enemies, had said?

His dark brows met. Memory and doubt touched his face. 'Sometimes, it was not.' Then he studied her face, finally gracing her with a smile. 'Henceforward, you will be my translator.'

Was he in jest? 'Then I have much more to learn.' They shared a smile.

Dancers filled the floor again and Gil shepherded her to a corner of the Hall, away from the crush and the noise, and they stood silent for a time. Finally, Valerie took a shaky breath. 'Tell me,' she began, 'about Castile.'

Gil's smile disappeared, as if the word brought memories he did not want to share. 'It is hard to explain.'

'You had said it was freezing and boiling. And yet, you long to return.'

'I spoke of the campaign,' he said. 'All campaigns are hard. The mountains were cold, but the plains were warm and dry.'

A hot, dry land. What could possibly grow in such a place? Her roses thrived on the dew of a summer morning, before the sun rose too high. 'It does not sound...welcoming.'

'Ah, but the palace, Alcázar, is a wonder. You will understand when you see it. Courtyards, gardens...you could live outside as easily as under a roof.'

Gardens. Perhaps this foreign land might hold one familiar joy.

She could see her own garden, clear, in her memory, knew every inch of it. She had left home in February and it was April now. She had missed seeing the periwinkles bloom. The bluebells would be next.

But she had planned to do so many things before now. The latticework where the roses climbed needed repair and the tunnel vine arbour, planted by her Castilian ancestor years ago, would soon leaf over. If only she could go home, just for a time. To stand and see the dappled sunlight filter through the vines…

She glanced at Gil again. He had smiled on her today. Perhaps, if she asked nicely… 'I, too, have a garden. Now that spring has come it needs care. If I might have your leave to go home, just for a visit—'

'No.' Abruptly he became again the harsh, fearsome man who frowned to see her. But he pulled her further away from the crowd and lowered his voice to a near whisper. 'You must not leave London.'

What had she said to cause such anger? 'I would seek the Queen's permission, of course.'

He shook his head, keeping her hands tightly gripped in his. 'Not even then. It is too dangerous. We have word that the Castilian and French are gathering ships to cross the Channel.'

Talk of war was hard for her to follow when she was thinking of her garden. 'I do not understand.'

He leaned in, his lips close enough to brush her cheekbone, and whispered in her ear, 'The enemy may try to invade our shores.'

Wide-eyed, she looked up and met his eyes. He nodded, silent, grim.

Shocked, she looked over at the whirling circle dancers, not really seeing them. The war, always safely distant, here? On English soil? Even in her precious garden? Such a thing was unimaginable.

But as she looked again at Gil, and then to Lancaster and to the priest, she could see what she had missed before. The tight lips. The furtive glances.

These were not men thinking of music and dance.

And still he held her hands, the warmth itself reassurance.

She looked back at Gil and squeezed his fingers, a silent answer. 'As you wish,' she said. 'I will remain here.'

He dropped her hands and they stood, silent, looking out at the dancers. Folly, somehow, to speak of ordinary things now. And yet, he stayed at her side, almost as if to lift a sword against the enemy, should they approach.

She looked back at the Queen, still smiling by her husband's side.

She does not know. Valerie's certainty caught her by surprise.

And only by chance that Valerie did not wear a smile as ignorant as the Queen's. Both women, who must submit to the will of their husbands, and yet for all her power, the Queen, alone in a country not her own, seemed somehow more helpless than Valerie.

For she was isolated behind walls of words she did not understand, her world translated by men with motives of their own. Did her husband seek to spare her worry? Or to prevent her from interfering? It did not matter. He had snatched her choice along with the knowledge.

She glanced up at Gil.

He had not told her to keep the news secret.

And she would not ask.

The Queen's household slept late the next day.

Valerie did not. She rose early to pace the corridor, looking out each window at the river below. How far was it to the sea? Two days' ride, on a fast horse. And if a boat could travel upstream, could it even reach London?

She touched the walls, aware for the first time how thick and strong they were. Would they be safe, even here?

Perhaps she should speak to Katherine first. But if Katherine, close as she was to the Duke, knew of this and had not spoken of it, she might warn Valerie to say nothing.

For a moment, she stood, torn between loyalty to her betrothed and to the Queen. But what difference would it make to the men if the Queen were told? Their preparations would be the same. It was only the women who must be kept in ignorance, as if they were blind and deaf, valued only for the body that lay below the neck.

That had been the life she knew. But a queen? Well, a queen deserved better.

Late in the morning, she found a quiet, private moment, without the other women, to speak. The priest was there and she was certain he would try to block her meaning, but she could not wait. Her Castilian was insufficient to convey this important news, but she could say enough to force him to speak the truth.

She began with compliments and pleasantries, a remembrance of the last night's joys, lulling the priest with smiles.

And then she changed her tone. 'Sadly,' she began, 'amidst such joy, it came to my ears that a fleet of Castilian and French ships may threaten our shores.'

The priest's flow of translation stopped. He turned to look at her, in horror.

Valerie met his eyes. 'You have already informed La Reina of this news, I am certain.'

The man's ruddy cheeks paled, a look more of guilt than fear. Yes, as she had thought, he had known the truth and kept from her what the woman should have been told. At her husband's command, no doubt.

The Queen looked from one to the other, then spoke to the priest, who muttered something. From the calm look on the Queen's face, he had conveyed nothing of what she had said.

So. Just as Valerie had suspected.

She paused. She still could keep the secret. And she should. An obedient wife would do so. If she told the Queen what she knew, there would be Gil's anger to face. But he was a man, free to come and go in the world. For all that she was a queen, Constanza, younger than Valerie and pregnant, was at the mercy of what the men around her were willing to share.

Today, Valerie could do something to change that.

'Father,' she said, 'perhaps you should try again.' Her tone of warning would need no translation. 'La Reina should know the *caballeros* may come here.'

The Queen looked at him sharply. *'Qué dice?'*

'Sobre la guerra...' And more words. Enough to bring a frown to her face, but not, Valerie thought, the whole truth.

With a pointed look at the priest, she spoke clearly. 'If you are unable to do so, I will do it myself, but I am certain your command of the language will more gently convey the truth than my few, blunt phrases. And please tell La Reina, *exactamente*, that since an invasion threatens, she and the babe would be safer in the country, away from London.'

She turned to the Queen then, keeping her eyes and her smile steady. The priest translated, seemingly accurately this time, for the Queen's eyes widened in fear, then her lips narrowed with resolve, and finally, she nodded with understanding,

'Gracias, señora,' she said, never taking her gaze from Valerie.

Another exchange between the Queen and the priest.

'La Reina is grateful for your loyalty,' he said, finally. 'And for the dedication that you, and your betrothed, have shown to the true throne of Castile. She will have My Lord of Spain find a suitable castle in the country. Will your husband allow you to stay and help as we move to safety?'

A welcome reprieve. At one time, Gil had insisted she serve the Queen. Now, the Queen's favour might shield her from his anger.

She sank into a deep, grateful curtsy. '*Gracias, Mi Reina*. I will ask him for permission to do so.'

The Queen smiled.

Chapter Eight

Bad enough that he was being forced to wed, Gil thought, as he strode through the corridor. Worse that he had been given a wife who could not be trusted to keep the secrets he had been careless enough to share.

Not only had she taken it upon herself to tell the Queen of their marriage, she had also apparently implied that the Castilian fleet was in sight of the coast. As a result, the terrified Queen had insisted that Lancaster send her entire household to the country. Instead of spending time on the island's defence, Gil had spent the morning sending messengers to Hertford, Higham Ferrers and Kenilworth castles to see which of them could shelter and defend the Queen and her ladies.

My Lord of Spain had not been pleased.

And now, the Lady Valerie was going to hear of it.

He entered the outer chamber of the Queen's quarters unannounced to see Valerie, on her knees, surrounded by trunks.

She did not look up.

'This chest contains La Reina's private altar and crucifix...' she began, pointing, as if giving directions to a servant. 'It must be moved with the utmost care and should packed in the first cart. She will want it as soon as we arrive so she can thank God for our safe journey.'

She turned to other items, as if expecting a servant to come and lift the chest.

But when he stood, speechless, she asked again. 'Come, quickly.'

Then she lifted her head, saw him and scrambled to her feet. 'Forgive me, my lord. I did not know it was you.' The woman who had confidently been giving orders to an unseen servant bowed her head and lowered her eyes.

His ire burst into words. 'When you become my wife, I do not expect you to share my every counsel with the Queen!'

The words rattled off the wall and she cringed. Her face, unguarded, reflected a moment of terror, as if she expected him to land a blow.

Quickly, she ducked her head again, bending a knee. 'I thought only to serve the Queen as faithfully as you serve her husband. I thought My Lord of Spain would want her protected in case…'

In case the worst happened.

Her reminder stopped his tongue. It *was* wise for the Queen to be moved to safety and he felt a bite of shame that neither he, nor the woman's husband, had thought of it.

He cleared his throat, struggling for calm. 'I see. That is true, yes.' Had he told her to keep her counsel? He could not remember now. And even if he had, no man should shout at his wife as he would at an ox that would not pull his plough.

She raised her eyes to his. 'Give me what punishment I deserve.'

'Punishment?' What did this woman take him for? Angry as he was that she had spoken without his permission, her exaggerated meekness seemed an accusation. It was as if despite his lifetime of striving for the ideals of knighthood, she could sense the darkness within him.

'No,' he said, 'there will not be... I do not mean...'

He paused to study her face. She had assumed her blank look again, impossible to read. When first he met her, she had scorned his outstretched hand and turned away as if she were a lady of the highest rank. He had thought her sad, but strong. Now, she cowered before him as if she were a dog he had kicked.

Well, given the way he had stomped into the room, bellowing at the top of this voice, he should not be surprised. No need to think she could sense some hidden monster in his soul when he had behaved like an fool.

He bowed his head, in a brief apology. 'I was for'wrought.' He could not blame his family for her fear. His own blustering missteps were reason enough. 'The morning has been spent in search of the best place for the Queen's household. In a day or two, we will know where you are to go.'

'The Queen will be grateful,' she said. 'As will I.' And still she did not raise her eyes.

The Lady Katherine had warned him of bad beginnings. He must take care not to lose his temper again. 'Look at me.' A gentler voice. 'Please.'

Startled, she raised her head, dark eyes

wide, looking into his. 'If you wish, in the future I will—'

'Do you find me so hard to look on?'

A shy smile. A touch of pink on her cheek she could not hide. 'I find you…' she swallowed '…pleasant to look on.'

Now, he was the one who could not keep a smile from his face. He took a step towards her.

She shrank away.

He paused. 'Do not fear me, Valerie.' As if he could command her feelings.

She kept her eyes on his, as if to prove she did not. 'I do not fear you.'

A brave lie. He had seen enough men prepare for battle to know. Or, perhaps he was wrong and she was only wary, like an animal ready to flee if threatened. 'Good.'

'I scarcely know you.'

'Nor I you.' And the more time he spent with her, the more she confused him. She could defy him to share information with the Queen, yet face to face, she was all meek subservience. 'Yet My Lord of Spain has matched us, so, it seems, we should…talk.' They had exchanged a few words last night, speaking for the first time of something beyond necessities. Even then, the talk had been of Castile and little else. A woman must expect some… wooing.

'As you wish.' No more.

'What shall we speak of?'

Now, puzzlement. 'You said you thought we should talk. I presumed you had something to say.'

What woman, invited to talk, ever remained silent? What did Lancaster do to make the Lady Katherine smile? But perhaps… Had he the courage to speak today? 'You asked before about my family.' There. He had given her another opportunity to ask.

A slight raising of her eyebrows. 'You have made it clear that is not something you wish to discuss.'

He detected no hint of suspicion in her words.

'Besides,' she continued, 'My Lord of Spain believes us worthy of each other. That is all I need to know.'

Relief. Reprieve. One day he must tell her himself, but not today. Not until she was less frightened of him.

'Better that, as your wife, I learn what pleases you. You must let me know, as you did today, when I do not.'

'What pleases me?' He did not know how

to answer the question. 'I am pleased when we are victorious, when my lord praises my prowess. And I will be pleased when we attain Castile.' He thought the word would bring light to her eyes. It did not. 'But I would learn of you, as well.'

A slight lift of the chin. As if she were the child, forced to fulfil his wishes. 'What would you like to know?'

'You seemed not eager to marry. Was it… something about me you did not like?'

She shook her head, without hesitation. 'As I recall, neither were you eager to wed.' A smile then. One that seemed to tease him. 'I should ask whether you objected to me.'

'No! Of course not. I meant to marry some day, of course. Just not…now.'

'Well, you see, I had married already. I did not think it necessary to do it again.'

He knew few women well and had never thought of how they spent their days, be they wives or widows. Would her life be different if she did not wed? 'If you had been allowed to remain a lady of dower, what would you do?'

'I would be on my lands. Tending to the crops and flocks.'

Dull work. The kind he had been glad to

avoid as a man of war. 'But when the work is done, what do you do then? Do you like chess?' Perhaps there was something she enjoyed and had feared he would not allow it. 'Or the hunt?'

She looked up at him, puzzled. 'How does that matter? The time you and I spend together will be in bed, not in play.'

What kind of marriage had she had with Scargill? Did he come home, bed her, and then leave with no more than a word?

Or was it worse than that?

He tried to remember what he knew of the man. He had certainly seen him raise his voice, and his hand, in anger. But to a woman...?

Something Gil could not imagine. But if it were true, it might explain her meek behaviour around him. He put the thought aside to join a lengthening list of things he did not want to speak about.

'Certainly, we will, uh...spend time outside the marital bed.' But now that she had raised it, the thought of bedding her flushed all logic from his mind. Heat gathered. His body leapt to attention.

He struggled to regain command. 'So, again, what do you like to do?' He hoped, desperately, that it would be something he knew something of. The Lady of Losford had despaired of his grasp of poetry.

Puzzlement. As if no one had ever asked her the question. And then, she paused, thinking, taking his question as genuine.

'I like to grow things,' she said, finally, with a nod of her head.

'Grow?' She had already spoken of crops. What could she mean now? 'Like herbs?'

Her cheeks reddened. 'Flowers.' A smile. Soft, involuntary. 'I like to grow flowers.'

'Flowers.' The word lay before him like a weapon he did not know how to wield. Well, she had asked of the growing things of Castile. He had not known how to answer then. Or now. He cleared his throat. 'And why do you like flowers?'

How witless he sounded. But at his interest, the dreamy smile on her face turned to joy. 'It seems God created them only to make us glad. The roses in my garden are so many beautiful shades of red and of white. And their scent...' She paused to inhale, as if smelling them still. 'The earliest ones will bloom soon, or should. If I could be there...'

Then, she remembered and her joy dimmed. 'But I know that is not possible.'

'I'm sorry,' he said, regretting the way he

had cut her off last night when she had asked
to go home. 'It is not.' *I have a garden*, she
had said. As precious to her, it seemed, as his
memories of Alcázar were to him.

And so again, she donned her dutiful smile.
'You spoke of the gardens of Alcázar. What
flowers grow there?'

'I am no gardener to know what the green
things are called, but I have not seen their
like here.'

'Forgive me. It is not for a warrior to call
the blossoms by their names.' Her determined
smile wobbled. 'My question was foolish.'

He put a hand on her shoulder, a gesture
he might have used to reassure a soldier. 'No.
It wasn't.'

He was the fool. Until he had seen the tiled
courtyards of Castile, he knew of gardens
only as gloomy places where dark secrets
were buried. 'I have been a man too close to
war and too far from…'

Home. As far from that haunted castle as
possible.

But this woman found joy in the earth,
could even coax something of beauty from
the soil. Could she do that for a home as well?
Make it one he did not want to flee?

She nodded, as if his touch had steadied

her. 'I will ask La Reina. She will know,' she said. 'And if there are no roses, can we take some with us when we go there?'

'We will not need to carry memories of England to Castile,' he said. 'Our gardens will be full of new plants.'

He let his hand slide down her arm, leaned forward, as if to reassure her.

She blinked. Her lips parted.

Just a little closer and, he could kiss her. He could claim what would rightfully be his. There was a smudge of dust on her nose and a lock of hair had escaped, the strands mixed brown and gold. But the rest remained damnably tucked beneath the widow's wimple, as if she still belonged to that other man.

He pushed the lock of hair aside and let his lips brush her cheek, then pulled her closer.

She lay unmoving in his arms, then whispered, 'The servants will return.'

Of course. Not here. Not now.

He let her go and rose, moving away to break the pull of her. What had happened? He had stormed into the room, angry at her disloyalty and then, his mind had been wiped clean of all thought except to make her his. No wonder he preferred war to love. The outcomes, and the terrain, were much more manageable.

Dangerous, this woman. He did not recognise himself around her. She was a knot he could not untangle and each time he tried, he only found himself further ensnared.

He had wasted valuable time here when he should have been planning for war. 'It is too soon to think of flowers,' he said, looking down at her, his frown firmly in place again. 'If we do not retake the throne, we will see no gardens at all in Castile.'

Again, she became the meek, joyless soul. 'Of course, my lord. I mean, Gil.'

She said his name by rote. He wished she would call him nothing at all. 'And be sure the Queen is prepared to move by week's end.'

'La Reina asked that I come with her household. May I have your permission to do so?'

Lancaster had said nothing of when they were to wed. In the meantime, it was better they stay apart. That way, he would let slip no more secrets. And in Hertford, she would be safely away from the court, where she might hear rumours of the Brewen past. 'Yes. Of course.'

As she had promised, the servants returned,

allowing him to escape, more confused than when he arrived.

He did not understand this woman at all. Worse, he did not understand himself when he was around her.

And so, while the men prepared to defend the coast, Valerie moved with chests, Castilians and pie bird to Hertford Castle, far enough from London so that, if the unthinkable happened, Castile's Queen would be out of harm's way.

Valerie sent a message, but did not see Gil again before they left. Word of the Castilian–French fleet had finally become known and rumours of war now filled the court.

The move had been intended to allow the household to live with a sense of peace and safety. Valerie, united again with a garden, was the only one who felt it. Once settled into the country home, she could snatch time alone to watch the purple fleur-de-lis emerge, day by day. Beauty that required no translation.

The Queen, heavier with child, spent even more time in prayer, no doubt pleading for God to spare her and her unborn child from the terrors of birth-bearing as well as the swords of the enemy. And by the panic in her ladies' voices Valerie guessed they chattered of what would happen if the pretender to the throne landed and found their hiding place.

At Hertford, they were even more isolated than they had been at the Savoy. Since London was two days' ride away, they received their news from the household's priests, who travelled regularly between the court and the country home. Valerie had no faith they spoke the truth.

Separately, Katherine was also travelling to London regularly and brought reports Valerie counted as more reliable, for they came, she assumed, from the Duke himself.

The purpose for Katherine's trips was, she explained, was to confer with Lancaster about the children. Was there another, more private reason she visited so often? Valerie was beginning to wonder. For when she did return to Hertford, Katherine spent most of her time with the children of John's first wife and her own, not with the Queen.

Both Katherine, and Constanza, preferred it that way.

And if, as Valerie was beginning to suspect, each woman ruled a separate realm of the man's life, it was no more than any wife, or mistress, could expect.

* * *

One evening in May, as the sky turned from blue to pink, Valerie and the Queen were trying again to teach words to each other. There was soft laughter when one got something right, or wrong. No, they hoped not to be in England for long. England was cold and *feo*. Castile was warm and *magnífico*.

And then, the Queen hushed them all and asked her favourite singer among her ladies for a song of home.

Even though Valerie had never been there, the music roused her as well. If she could speak the tongue, if the gardens were beautiful as Gil had promised, could she find peace there? Or, a year from now, would she, too, be hearing songs of home and feel as isolated and alone as these women?

Constanza lay quietly, eyes closed, and the pain seemed to lessen with the melody. Perhaps the music reminded her of home, childhood, of a time of safety. Did she sleep? Valerie could not say, but she seemed to find a moment's peace.

And then, her face turned rigid.

She clutched her belly and groaned, then gasped, trying to get the words free. '*Mi niño...*'

The song broke off. The Castilian ladies surrounded their lady, turning their backs on Valerie.

She rose, not knowing what to do. She had never borne a child. Knew nothing of what came now. Was the baby to come immediately?

The midwife had been called to a birth half a day's ride away. But Katherine was here. Katherine had borne four children and served the Duke's duchess.

'I will get Lady Katherine,' she called, hoping Constanza would hear and understand.

A muffled response. Did the Queen protest? Hard to hear amidst the cries and whispers and the screech of the pie bird.

She ran through the halls, to the rooms Katherine occupied with her own children, bursting in without introduction.

'La Reina. She is in pain. The baby...' What a fool she was, to not even be able to speak of it.

Katherine rose, without a word, and walked into the corridor.

Valerie followed her, but when they entered the Queen's quarters, the ladies turned to look, but did not move away.

'Let me see her,' Katherine said.

She stepped forward, forcing the ladies to part. Valerie stayed nearby, hoping that by coming closer to the birth, God might understand how much she, too, wanted a child.

And so, she was close enough to see a flash in the Queen's eyes. It was more than pain. Was it hate? Could the Queen, too, think that Katherine and her husband...?

La Reina took an easy breath. And then another.

The ladies looked at each other, nervous.

Katherine took the woman's hand, squeezed it, then placed a damp cloth on her brow. 'Rest now. The babe does not come yet.' A smile. A calm voice. Enough to allow the Queen to close her eyes.

Only when they left the room did Valerie see Katherine's unguarded face. The reassuring smile she had worn for the Queen was gone.

'Are you certain,' Valerie whispered, 'that the babe will not come now?'

'I cannot be sure, but the child is not due until June, another month or more.'

Valerie did not need to ask how Katherine knew with such certainty when the heir was to be born. 'But couldn't the babe come sooner? And if it comes too early…' Even Valerie knew the dangers of that.

Katherine touched her arm. 'Go to London. Tell John to send the midwife who assisted the Lady Blanche.' Her aura of calm had returned. 'I believe that we will need her.'

'And you?' Surprised that Katherine would not go to John herself.

'I must stay to help.'

Sensible, since Valerie could be of little use at all. 'I will leave at first light.'

Katherine nodded, her pursed lips betraying her worry.

Valerie touched the woman's arm, attempting comfort. 'If you have a private message, something you would like me to take to My Lord of Spain…'

Katherine blinked and started.

Were things not as she suspected? She bit her tongue, fearing she had said too much.

But then, Katherine looked around, to be certain they could not be overheard, and her face softened. 'Please tell him that I will do everything I can for his Queen. And I will care for the child as if it were my own.'

Something deeper than pleasure, then, between Katherine and Lancaster. Something that allowed Katherine to serve the man's wife because in doing that, she could serve him.

She nodded. 'I will be sure he knows.'

Katherine's face softened, seeing a friend who recognised the truth and did not judge her for it.

And Valerie saw everything she knew about love and marriage laid out before her. Duty within marriage. Passion beyond it. Strange allies, Constanza and Katherine, wife and mistress, united in their loyalty to the same man, each carrying her own pain. And Valerie the bridge between them.

A reminder of all the reasons she had hoped to remain aloof from marriage. And yet, she felt a strange envy for Katherine, and even for her late husband. Each had touched passion she would never know.

And Gil? While Valerie was the dutiful wife, what woman would earn his love? One with fair hair and blue eyes, no doubt. Valerie lacked both, as Scargill had frequently reminded her. Her hair, at least, she could cover.

She embraced Katherine quickly. 'I will fetch the midwife myself and bring her here as quickly as I can.'

Valerie's own promise. To both women.

* * *

Two days later, back at Lancaster's London palace, Valerie waited as the page announced her, then entered the room, still rehearsing the words Lady Katherine had told her to say to Lancaster.

But it was Gil, standing next to his liege, who met her eyes first. Surprise touched his face.

'Do you find me so hard to look on?' he had asked. In truth, she loved to rest her eyes on him. The shock of dark hair that fell across his forehead, the strong eyebrows that protected eyes the pale blue of a winter sky, and, the few magical times she had seen him smile, it was as though he knew a secret and if she just followed him, even as far as Castile, she, too, might discover a wondrous land.

Today, he did not smile. Clearly, he was neither expecting, nor longing, to see her again.

'What is it?' Lancaster's voice jarred her. She had forgotten she was not alone in the room with Gil. 'Lady Katherine? The Queen?'

Of course, he would ask after Katherine first.

She dipped a curtsy. 'Both were well when

I left, but the Queen has had a difficult time. Lady Katherine believes the babe will come soon. There is a midwife at Hertford, but the Lady Katherine asked that you send for Elyot.'

There was a stricken look on his face for a moment.

'Who is Elyot, my lord?' Gil asked.

'Elyot, the wise woman. She attended the Lady Blanche. More than once.' Some pain still lingered in his voice, when he spoke of his dead wife.

'Do you know where to find her, Your Grace?' she asked.

'Leicester,' Lancaster said, turning to Gil. 'Go. Bring her back.'

Every time she had mentioned his home, he had resisted. And today was the same. 'There are still preparations before the expedition sails. I should stay to—'

'No.' The Duke again. 'My heir is more important.' He paused for a moment. 'Besides, this will allow you to visit your lands. I know you have…neglected them to serve me.'

So, it was not only that he did not want to speak to her of his home and family. He seemed to want nothing to do with it at all.

But though Gil could refuse her, he could

not refuse his lord. 'I will deliver the woman to Hertford,' Gil said. 'And return within a fortnight.'

The Duke looked at Valerie. 'Have we enough time?'

June, Katherine had said. Still some weeks away. 'I believe so, but we should bring the woman as quickly as we can.'

The Duke nodded and turned to Gil. 'A brief visit. Time enough to give final instructions to your steward while the midwife prepares to travel.'

Then, they began to speak of ships and ports and men and ambassadors. A dizzying set of plans. She could not follow them all, but it seemed that the expedition was to sail for La Rochelle within weeks. Were they to fight the enemy fleet on the way? She was not sure.

But she did hear, clearly, the last. That Gil was to lead an invasion of Castile. Perhaps as soon as the next month.

She averted her eyes, pretending not to listen. La Reina would be glad of the news, she was certain, but the last time she had carried word of war to the Queen, Valerie had incurred the wrath of her husband and the Duke.

But this time, Gil looked over at her, pride

in his eyes, and then exchanged looks with My Lord of Spain.

'Your Queen,' Gil began. 'She should know. Of the plans.'

My Lord of Spain waved a hand in acknowledgment. 'I will send word.'

'Lady Valerie can carry your message to the Queen,' Gil said. 'I will ride for the midwife at first light.'

'No!' The word slipped out before she could stop it. 'Not without me.'

Silent, both men looked at her. Disbelief touched Lancaster's face.

Anger masked Gil's. 'I must move quickly,' he said. 'She will slow me down.'

She straightened her shoulders. She was not yet this man's wife. And she had made a promise. 'I was not carried here on a litter, my lord. Give me a swift horse and I am prepared to leave immediately.'

Still, Gil protested. 'My lord, I do not want, I mean...'

He did not want her to see his home. Of that she was certain. But she had promised Katherine that she would bring the wise woman herself. It seemed to be the one thing she could give, to Katherine and to the Queen. She must not fail.

She squared her shoulders and faced the Duke. 'I can tell Elyot of the Queen's condition on our journey, so she will be able to act without delay as soon as we reach Hertford.'

The Duke's frown eased and he nodded. 'All that is possible must be done to ensure the safety of my son.'

'And of the Queen,' she said, softly. But she and Katherine, it seemed, must be the ones to worry about his Queen, grasping her belly in pain, in what might soon be her birthing bed.

But Lancaster was thinking of neither woman, rather of that land far away. 'When we return to Castile, we must show the people that the succession is assured. All must go well.'

Gil did not protest again, but looked at her, sternly. 'We must make twenty miles a day.'

'I am not infirm, my lord,' Valerie said, though her legs ached at the thought of clinging to a horse for another week. 'But I will need a new mount.' She looked at the Duke. 'I rode from Hertford to London in less than two days. The horse deserves a rest.'

Now Gil frowned indeed. The journey was near thirty miles, fair proof that she would not delay him on the way. 'All will be ready.'

She dipped a bow to the Duke.

'And, Lady Valerie…'

She looked up to see the Duke's eyes on her. 'Yes, my lord?'

'When you see her, give the Lady Katherine my most profound thanks.'

'She asked me…' she swallowed '…to tell you that she would do everything she could for your Queen. That she would care for the child as if it were her own.'

And if she had wondered at the truth before, she saw it now on the face of My Lord of Spain. For at those words, he looked not like a king, but like John, a man who might be the father of Katherine's next child.

She looked at Gil for help and saw, in his dismay, the confirmation of all she had thought.

'And your thoughts to the Queen as well,' Gil added, hastily.

'Yes, yes,' the Duke said, as if it were an afterthought. 'The Queen as well.'

The Duke should have remembered his Queen, yes, but Gil spoke as if he expected the man to care for his wife as much as for his mistress. That was nothing a wife should expect.

Or even hope for.

Certainly, when Gil looked at her again, no tenderness remained on his face. 'Be ready at dawn,' he said sharply.

Chapter Nine

The speed of travel saved Gil from wasting his breath in chatter. Scargill's widow did, indeed, slow them down. Or perhaps it was the number of men in the escort or the lame horse which had to be replaced or the swollen river that forced them to detour to find an easier ford.

Still, they would reach Leicestershire too quickly. And when they did, he would be forced, finally, to tell Valerie something of his life.

What would she think of him then?

'The Duke must trust you very much,' Valerie said, when they paused at noon on the second day.

It was the first time she had acknowledged his appointment to lead the invasion and, despite all, her praise pleased him. He had sought this honour for years, the hope of it resting beside the tile he carried from the gardens, a constant reminder. 'My Lord of Spain knows that no other man in his retinue is more committed to regaining Castile. As leader of the force, I will make sure we attain our goal.'

'I was not thinking of Castile.'

He looked at her, puzzled. 'What then?'

'It was you he trusted to bring the wise woman safely to the Queen.'

How like a woman, to think of small matters. Did she not understand how singular the task that lay before him? 'My time would be better spent preparing to retake the throne.'

'But nothing can be more precious to him than the life of his wife and child. Not if he is to be King in deed.'

He shrugged, uneasy now. The heir was important, yes, but he had wanted nothing of this trip, least of all being forced to return to the Castle of the Weeping Winds. 'I should be planning alternate routes to Castile, not riding halfway to York to fetch a particular midwife because this Spanish woman is fearful of doing what she was born to do.'

Valerie jerked, as if he had slapped her. 'You speak harshly. Childbirth is part of God's purpose, but there is no certainty that the babe or the mother will survive.'

Now he was the one who felt the flush of shame. 'I have not fathered a child.' No excuse. Any fool knew as much. This woman might even have lost a child. 'I should not have spoken so.' And what if the Queen were to die? What would happen then? 'Is her life at risk?'

'The Lady Katherine thinks so.'

A strange answer. 'And you?'

She was silent and looked away before she met his eyes again. 'I have never been with child. I do not know.'

'Never?' She had said she had no children, but he had thought…well, as she said, many babes did not survive.

She shook her head. 'I should have told you. You have a right to know that before we…' She averted her eyes. 'You might want another bride.'

He thought of Cecily and Marc's son. He had dreamed of siring such a boy. Some day. 'Are you…barren?'

The very word seemed to unlock a secret pain. 'I do not know.'

He knew little of such things. But the fault could lie with either man or woman, he had heard. 'Did Scargill have other children?'

The edge of her mouth twitched in a sort of smile. 'You would know better than I.'

And he had known nothing at all. 'I knew little of the man's…habits.' A rueful smile. 'As I proved so painfully when first we met.'

Her smile, and a shake of the head, in answer.

She was difficult to read, this woman. By turns, he thought her cold and hard, then meek and so submissive she seemed to disappear. And then, he would glimpse a woman who might laugh at life. Even at herself.

And, probably, at him, when he deserved it. 'I was rude to question you.' Closer to the earth of home, he seemed to lose his grip on the chivalry he so coveted, at once prattling of his devotion to his lord and acting like the most churlish peasant to the woman who would be his wife. The Earl of Losford would have reached for the rod had he acted so. 'Of course we will wed.'

And though he had said it to reassure her, he felt a surge of conviction, more certain than he had known that this was to be.

But she did not smile to hear it. Instead, she looked at him as if he had no more sense than one of the chickens, who stood in the pouring rain as if it were sunshine. 'But it is only right that you should know. Would you buy a horse without inspecting his teeth and his forelegs?'

'A woman is not a horse.' It was his own guilt that argued. She had been forced to pledge herself to him knowing nothing of his past. And, so far, he had lacked the courage or the honour to tell her.

'But marriage is for the getting and raising of children,' she said. 'If it…if I cannot…' Forthright as she had been, she could not speak the words.

Now, he felt angry that she should even think such a thing. He had wanted a son, yes, but despite his desires, perhaps God had chosen to give him a barren wife and spare the world another child who carried the Brewen blood. 'We will speak no more of it.'

She opened her mouth, as if to protest, then pursed her lips firmly together. 'As you wish.'

The words were submissive, yet he was certain that she thought him a fool.

He had never been easy with women and knew little of them, except for the family of the Earl of Losford. Before they died, the Earl and his wife seemed happy and Cecily and Marc had defied a king for their love. Even the Duke had been besotted with his Blanche, all the more reason it was understandable that he could not revere his current wife in the same way.

And his own mother had been at constant war, it seemed, with her brothers, who would prey on the populace, then retreat behind the castle walls, untouchable.

He rose, helped Valerie to mount and then took his seat. 'When you see the Castle of the Weeping Winds, you will know more of the "horse" who is to be your husband.'

He spurred his mount ahead, so she could ask no questions. He could not hide his family's past much longer. Better she hear it from him. And after she learned even a portion of the truth, she might be the one to reject him. They had not yet consummated their union. Even the church would have to agree the betrothal could be broken.

Then, he might be free, again, to pursue Castile alone, as he had always planned.

The thought did not bring him comfort.

Valerie knew that Gil did not want to return to the Wolford lands. When she saw the Castle of the Weeping Winds, she knew why, at least in part.

The building was a hulking, empty shell.

Chunks of stone had fallen from the walls, leaving holes like wounds. Broken shutters no longer protected the battlements where archers might stand, leaving empty spaces like eyes gouged out. The few attendants who greeted them moved like ghosts.

The steward handles it, he had said. She would have fired the man.

The steward in question, shocked that he would have to find sleeping accommodations for a woman as well as Sir Gil and his small retinue, barely took time for a proper welcome before he scurried off, leaving her in the gloomy anteroom while Gil saw to the men and the horses.

No one will come, he had said. Now she knew why. No one was left.

When he came back into the Hall, she saw no smile, no sentiment on his face. Any memories he had of this place were not happy ones. No wonder he longed for Castile.

'So your family does not live here.' No longer a question. She was certain now—no mother, no sister, no one who cared for it lived in this hollow, empty place.

He shook his head. 'They are dead.'

How long had this place stood empty? A garden could go to seed so quickly. How fast could a house fall to ruin?

She parted her lips to ask, then paused. His expression did not invite questions.

'The steward will make the master's rooms habitable for you tonight,' he said.

'And for you?' She was grateful he would not seek to share her bed yet.

'I will sleep with the men. In the Hall.'

As fighting men so often did, stretched on thin blankets, circling the communal hearth.

She thought with longing of her own small, snug home and garden, imbued with the love of generations. For nearly ninety years, the roots of the roses had grown, deep and strong, then bearing blossoms that covered the lattice work as thickly as a woven tapestry covered castle walls.

If only they could live here instead of going to Castile, she knew she could make these cold walls welcoming.

But she had not come here because of her own future, but that of La Reina and her child. 'Where will we find the wise woman?'

'I have sent someone to bring her from town.' He turned, as if to leave. 'The steward will show you to the room as soon as it is ready.'

Weary as she was after endless days on the horse, she was tempted to retire to the bed he offered, but she had been handed a husband and the life that went with him. She would not let him run from her again.

'Wait!' Her voice was loud enough not to be ignored.

He looked back, the surprise clear on his face.

Would he raise his hand because she interrupted? Not with his men so close. She must speak now. 'If we are to be married, this will be my home.'

'I told you. We will not be here.'

'Even when we live with the court. Even if...' She gasped at her mistake, not realising until the word escaped how deeply she wanted to stay. A pause, and then she rushed ahead. 'Even *when* we go to Castile.'

She donned her contrite expression, hoping he would not shout at her for her doubt, then rushed to speak some words of appeasement. 'And we *will* go to Castile. I know.'

Some remembered pain gripped him, sharp at the corners of his eyes. Her fear ebbed. It seemed that neither the man's heart nor his home had seen comfort in a long time.

Her voice turned soft. 'This is the land you hold, the land that will belong to...' Could she risk the words? 'Our son. I would see it.'

A moment's silence. She tried to read his face. Surprise? Anger? Scargill had always lashed out immediately. This man seemed always to reflect first.

A sigh. A shrug. 'The steward can show you.' He shifted his weight, as if the conversation was over.

He could face a sword, it seemed, but not this. What was here, in these walls, in this earth, that he feared?

'Not the steward! You.' Her voice, not as strong as she had hoped. 'I want *you* to show it to me.'

She held out her hand.

Her fingers trembled and she tried to hold her arm steady as she met his gaze. His blue eyes seemed at once to burn and freeze her, leaving her unable to speak or move.

If he touches my hand, if I feel his skin on mine—

But he did not stretch out his hand.

She let her shaking arm drop and looked down at the floor, feeling the heat of shame rush to her cheeks. He did not want a wife.

He did not want *her*.

'Very well. Come.'

And she had to take quick steps to follow him out of the room.

Valerie wondered, as they walked the corridors, whether she might have learned more if she had been guided by the steward. *Here is the hall. Here are the stables.* He volunteered little more than the name of each chamber. No mention of childhood memories. Not a word about his family.

Who had lived in these empty rooms? What had life been like for Gil at five or six? This was his home, the place he had lived as a child, and yet she had heard more feeling in his voice when he spoke of Castile.

'You will learn what kind of horse will be your husband', he had promised. And yet these empty walls only deepened the mystery.

'It has been a long time,' she began, softly, 'since anyone lived here.'

'Yes.'

The steward might have managed the tenants, but he was a terrible housewife. Perhaps he kept his own quarters tidy, but dust, spider webs, even birds' nests filled the castle's corners. What furnishings that remained were rude. She saw not even a decorative candlestick or a threadbare tapestry to grace the halls. Of course, no careful steward should waste time and money to keep empty rooms ready for a master who never visited. 'Was it like this when you were a child?'

'Nearly so.' There was a grim set to his

lips. 'When I came to Losford Castle I knew nothing of courtly arts.'

'And you had no brothers or sisters?'

'My brother became a monk. I have not seen him in years.'

She understood. It was the way of things.

Finally, they reached the master's room. The servants had done what they could. The dust was gone. The bed, covered with sheet and blanket, looked as simple as one in an almshouse.

And yet, it was a bed. One they might share some day.

She looked away. A marital bed had never been a pleasant place for her.

He walked to the window, gazing out, and did not look back at her when he finally spoke. 'You told me that I should know what I am getting,' he said. 'That no man should buy a horse without inspecting his teeth and his forelegs.'

The words sounded colder than she had intended. 'Yes.'

He turned, finally, and faced her. She tried to read him, uncertain whether she had angered or saddened him with her questions.

'And you should know the same.' He gestured for her to sit.

A small stool stood beside the bed. She ran her hand over it, to see that the dust had been cleared, sat and clasped her hands, waiting.

He did not speak immediately, but stood, first looking out of the window, then letting his gaze take in the chamber and whatever memories lurked here. Finally, he met her eyes and took a breath.

'My mother was a Brewen.'

Brewen. The very name seemed evil. She had heard the tales, too wild to be believed, of things that had happened before she was born: men who had extorted money, raped women, and priests who had disappeared, never to be seen again...

'But that was years ago,' she said, as if time could erase such wickedness.

'It began before this King sat on the throne, before we went to war with France. Full forty years and more ago.'

Yet men still crossed themselves when the name was spoken. And now, this man, one who carried that blood, would be her husband and share her bed. She tightened her fingers, as if to pray. 'Tell me.'

He looked at her, silent for a moment before he began.

'My Brewen grandfather had seven sons and one daughter. The girl was my mother.'

Gil hated the telling, hated reliving a past he wanted only to forget. But no one else had told her the truth, so he must be the one.

Seven Brewen sons. Too many for the land to support.

He had known, even as a child, that his family carried shame. Youngest of the line, his Brewen mother had married a Wolford, but still could not escape. His father had died when he was young and Gil had lived with his mother, still in the Brewen home.

They had called it the Castle of the Weeping Winds. Blood stained the walls and watered the ground.

Certainly, his family's sins were still buried here. But he would not speak of that, even now.

His grandfather had maintained the pretence of respectability, but Gil had seen his uncles come and go at all hours, retreating to the protection of the castle walls when the law came too close. Only one, who had become a priest, appeared to have escaped the curse.

The family had turned to crime a generation, even two, before that. Those were the years before the current King had solidified his power, before a man could earn a fortune in ransoms from fighting the French. In that time of unrest, it had been easy for a man to make his own law.

His mother had told him that her brothers were righteous men, that they were standing up against corrupt churchmen, so he did not know, exactly, all they had done. So it was not until he left home to foster at Losford that he discovered fully what it meant to be a Brewen.

He had wondered, over the years, why such a powerful man had taken him on. Later, when he knew the way of things, he learned that one of his uncles, perhaps more, had fought beside the King in France, their crimes pardoned because they helped win the glorious victory at Crecy.

Even outlaws could be useful to a king.

And so, the Earl had taken him in at the request of the King, no doubt thinking to remove him as far as possible from the bad influence of his family. But when Losford himself wasn't in the room, the other boys, the squires, even the knights ostracised him, refusing to see to his training, muttering that they did not want to teach him to swing a sword that he might use to run them through.

He carried Brewen blood. That was enough.

Gil's younger brother had retreated to the monastic life, perhaps to pray for the redemption of his uncles' souls. Gil chose the salvation of war, a way to prove his honour and escape to a foreign land.

As a squire serving Losford in France, he had that chance. In every action, he adhered to the code of chivalry. When some squires might pocket a coin or a bauble before turning over the rest, he never did. In the midst of battle, some knights might kill a man who had fallen, rather than taking him alive, ruled by fear more than greed. Gil did not. He would hold to honour, he decided, even at the cost of his own life, for without respect, he would rather abandon this existence.

Gradually, among those who fought beside him, the taunts faded. His own deeds grew larger in memory than his family's and he was knighted at a younger age than most of his peers.

Still, after the Earl of Losford died in France and unwelcome peace returned, Gil had to return to England. That was when Marc, a Frenchman who knew nothing of the Brewens, had taken him on and taught him more of fighting.

These were years of peace and Gil did not want peace.

So he joined Lancaster's service and returned to the Continent. After the battles in Castile came Aquitaine, Calais, Harfleur, Abbeville, Cognac, Limoges, and more. He stayed as far away from England as he could for as long as he could. And if peace came again? Then he would find another way to fight, in Italy or the Ottoman war.

But while he was away, one by one, his remaining uncles died: taken by the plague, by a river in flood, by a fall from his horse. One, they suspected, had been killed by the hand of one of his victims, though no one questioned too closely. Not one of them had spawned sons. So when his own mother died, the castle, the shameful legacy of all the Brewen blood, had come into his hands, an unwanted burden. He was finished with England, ready for a life in a place that knew nothing of his past and only of his own reputation.

He would not have returned at all, would never have seen this crumbling castle again if it had not been for Lancaster's promise of a home in Castile and the need to go back to England to prepare. He had thought it worth the risk, for it meant the chance to live in a place that knew only *El Lobo*.

And had never heard the name Brewen.

Gil had not looked at her, the whole of the time he had spoken, gazing into the past. He spoke as though to himself, for he had never been able to share the pain of it with anyone else.

And he could not face her still, wondering what she must think, now that she knew.

Still, he had not, could not, tell her all. Could tell no one of the things still buried in the earth…

Our Castle of the Weeping Wind, his mother had called it. Now, so empty that only the wind remained.

And even that wind could not blow away the disgrace.

Chapter Ten

Gil turned to face her, finally, expecting to see fear or disgust in her gaze, and yet it seemed nothing in the expression on her small, serious face had changed. Had she heard him at all?

'Now you know,' he said. He should have told her long ago, as soon as he realised her ignorance. Instead, they had stumbled into a betrothal neither had wanted. 'So you may ask the church to free you from this marriage. There must be a way. It is your right.'

He waited, expecting her to rise, to flee, to break the bonds that bound them and leave them both as they had been before. Yet the thought did not bring the relief he expected.

Instead, she shook her head, stood and reached for his hand. This time, she did not wait for him to take hers. Instead, she grasped both his hands in hers, more a blessing than a caress, and held them, tightly, between her palms.

'Oh, my husband, do you think you are the only one who has walked with pain?'

The heat of her hand on his, the look of forgiveness in her eyes, hit him as strongly as a blow. But instead of the agony of a wound, he was filled with the warmth and comfort of a fire in winter.

Was this what a wife could give?

He pulled his hands from hers, not to escape, but so that he could trail his fingers across her cheek. Surrounded by her widow's wimple, her face seemed light and luminous, dark eyes, pale skin, parted lips soft and sympathetic. He could not say she smiled, no. But her expression was more true, more real, than any of the smiles she had donned to disguise her feelings.

Now she knew the shame of who he was and, instead of recoiling in fear, she had reached to touch him.

His fingers bumped against the dark cloth covering her hair and he cupped her cheeks in his hands. She did not pull away, or look down, but as the heat of his hands settled on her skin, her eyes closed, her lips parted, she took a breath…

And he kissed her.

Her lips warm and soft. A moment in which she melted against him, the heat of her body, his, a promise, acceptance that cared nothing for the past.

His hands slid away from her face to her shoulders, then he pulled her close. She leaned against him, trusting in his touch, and he tightened his arms, wishing her gown, his tunic, everything that separated them would disappear.

And then, suddenly, he held a stiff, cold woman in his arms. She did not pull away, no, she was too obedient for that, but the comfort he had craved was gone. The fire he had wanted to spark sputtered like a flame on wet wood.

He set her away from him, with stiff arms and saw the flash of fear on her face. The truth.

She had said all was well and offered her comfort but, it seemed, only because it was her duty as a wife.

For now that she knew him as a Brewen, she feared him more than she had feared *El Lobo*.

* * *

For a moment, Valerie forgot.

She reached for him without fear, wanting to ease his pain. And when he kissed her, she had been a different woman, one who might join with him in joy.

And then, her body remembered what it was like to be taken. Remembered and responded, emptied of everything except the need to endure.

Now she had displeased him.

He rose. Moved away, further than an arm could reach. 'You fear me.' Not anger. Sorrow.

The edge of a laugh escaped. 'No. I do not.' After Scargill no man could frighten her.

'Is that a lie?'

She shook her head. 'It is true.'

It was her own feelings she feared.

There had been a rush, a yearning to join, to be a part of this man. Physical, yes, and worse. As if she might feel something for him.

And wanted him to feel something for her in turn.

As he studied her, she wondered whether, despite all she knew, that might be possible.

'I think,' he said, finally, 'that it is time to lay aside your mourning garb.'

Startled, she touched the wimple hiding her hair. Swathed in dark garments, she had worn the public protection of grief as a shield. The clothes, and the grief, both lies, a way to stay untouchable.

But she was no longer only a widow, but about to be another man's wife. Now, suddenly, the cloth covering her hair, neck and throat seemed to be choking her.

She nodded yes and tugged on the fabric, but it did not slip away easily. He drew closer and lifted his hand to push it aside. Near enough now that she caught the scent of him, a faint echo of herbs and earth.

She closed her eyes and leaned into him again. Hoping. Waiting…

The cloth dropped away and sweet, fresh air caressed her.

'Brown,' he whispered. 'Your hair is brown.'

She bit her lip. 'You wanted a fair-haired wife.' As she had feared.

He shook his head and threaded his fingers through her hair, then trailed them, light on her ear, his palm cupping her cheek again. 'I just wanted to know.' His breath, warm, close…

And his lips met hers again.

For a moment, she stiffened. This was the way her husband had begun. Moving in, over-powering her, so that she could not escape even were she to struggle.

She had learned not to struggle.

But this man's arms, though strong, were gentle. His touch spoke of protecting her from harm, not pummelling her into submission.

And now, her body, instead of becoming stiff to resist or limp to acquiesce became alive, moving to him, with him, as if a kiss might be something they could do together, not something that was done *to* her.

Was there wind? Sun? Was it day? Night? Nothing but him and his lips, for a long, slow, time...

And then, parted, gently, as if waking from a pleasant dream. A breath. A sigh. Even a smile.

And opening her eyes to see the same on his face.

A fierce, unfamiliar feeling stole her breath. Not desire, exactly, but hope. Hope that—

'My lord, the midwife is here.'

Valerie stumbled. Even Gil seemed caught speechless. The Queen. While she had been kissing her betrothed, both the Queen and Lady Katherine were waiting, each in her own kind of pain, for Valerie to return with the wise woman.

She wrestled with her wimple, but it would not go back into place. 'Take me to her,' she said, to the wide-eyed page. 'She must know the Queen's condition.'

Gil put a hand at her back. A pause. 'We leave in the morning,' he said. 'And we will not come here again.'

She fled the chamber, calling herself a fool.

She had acted as if she had learned nothing in all her nineteen years, as if all those horrible days, and worse nights, of the months before Scargill had left for war could be forgotten.

She had survived the pain by becoming numb to it, by teaching herself not to feel. Not to care. She had learned it well enough that no man would ever be able to hurt her again.

Even when Gil had handed her the scarf, proof her husband had betrayed her as well as beaten her, she had felt nothing. Her husband and her feelings, now both dead. Hope, desire, all those passions were well behind her.

Or so she thought.

But now, she must put aside all thoughts of her husband so that she could tell Elyot all she knew of the Queen's condition.

They left the next morning for Hertford. She did not see him alone again.

Gil delivered the midwife, who attended the Queen immediately. La Reina was still uncomfortable, Valerie told him, but there had been no new pains.

News he could deliver to Monseigneur d'Espagne without fear of distracting him from the military planning.

With the Queen safe, for the moment, he waited for Valerie to speak of his family. Or of their kiss. Instead, all seemed as it had been before, her wimple and her smile both firmly in place.

But as he was about to leave for London, a summons came. He and Valerie were to present themselves to the Castilian Queen.

'Why would she want to see us?' he whispered to Valerie, as they walked through the corridor, following one of the Queen's other ladies. He was learning to adjust his stride to hers, but still, she would break out in a run beside him.

'No doubt,' she began, doubling her steps, 'she wants to express her thanks.'

They paused before the closed door. She brushed the hair out of his eyes and straightened his sleeve. Small, comforting gestures, ones that might be witnessed, and yet, ones that made him feel as if they were married indeed.

And she the woman who had given herself to his kiss.

The door opened.

He served her husband, which meant he served the Queen as well, but somehow, he felt as if he had been summoned to the enemy camp. Valerie knew the woman well and he was strangely glad to have her by his side, as if she could shield him from harm.

La Reina's expression did not comfort him. She seemed to have aged years in the weeks since he had seen her in London.

Valerie dipped a curtsy.

Gil bowed. 'My Lord of Spain asked that I send you his warmest greetings and tell you he looks forward to the day you may return to London.'

Had he become such a liar? *And the Queen as well*, Lancaster had said, when Gil reminded him. Well, he did not say what words to use.

An interpreter sat at her side, but she did not wait for the Castilian translation before she shrugged, as if she knew exactly how inconsequential the words were.

'You are to wed Lady Valerie?' The interpreter's voice. The Queen's question.

He glanced at Valerie, then back to the Queen. A strange beginning. 'Yes, Your Grace.'

'La tratarás bien.'

'You will be good to her,' the translator said.

Not a question. A command.

He smiled. At the Queen, at Valerie, at the world in general. This, he could promise. 'I will, Your Grace.'

And yet Valerie looked to the ground again. Was she shy? Or did she have doubts, now that she knew the truth?

But the Queen had nodded, satisfied. Now she had a whispered conference and then her translator spoke again. 'You lead men to Castile.'

'Yes, Your Grace.' Surprising that she knew. Had her husband written? Or had Valerie shared the news? 'My Lord of Spain has given me the honour of commanding the expedition to Castile.'

'When?' The Queen's own voice. She had learned a few words of English from Valerie, it seemed.

He swallowed. 'When we hear from the King of Portugal, later this summer—'

'Ships to sail now. Not to Castile?'

He opened his mouth. Closed it. And silently cursed Lancaster and the priest Gutierrez. They had tried to keep the news from her, but it was too late for that.

Next to him, Valerie stood with head bowed and hands clasped, looking like a nun in prayer. Or like a conspirator, caught.

'Not this time, Your Grace. This is only a small force, going to relieve the siege at Thouars.' Pembroke's task was much more modest, perhaps the reason he had resented Gil.

The Queen looked at Valerie, who nodded. Had he confirmed news she had shared? If so, he had just proven her loyalty to the Queen. No small matter for those who lived in the shadow of a throne.

'No a Castilla?' The Queen herself spoke to him, the disappointment of her dashed hopes shimmering in the words. Perhaps she had hoped Valerie was wrong. Or that plans had changed again.

'Not yet, Your Grace. We hope by July.' How much should he tell her of diplomacy and invasion plans? 'With permission from the King, we can go through Portugal.'

Her expression, a mixture of pain and disgust. 'I did not marry the King of Portugal.'

'No, Your Grace.' How easy it must seem, to ride to war, when you knew nothing of men and ships and making certain you would not be attacked on the way to your objective. 'I, too, am eager to embark.'

'*Mi señor, el Rey…*forgot?'

The words an echo of his own fears. The King was ageing, the Prince was ill and Lancaster was pulled away from the affairs of Castile. Normandy, Aquitaine—there were battles on all sides. Some days, there were too many commanders. Other days, there seemed to be none at all.

'He has not.' Now, with clenched jaw. 'Nor have I.'

He must prove it. To her, to Valerie, to himself.

'My Lord of Spain gave me the honour of making certain we regain Castile because he knows that no man is more dedicated to that end.' He put a hand into his pocket and pulled out the stone he carried with him always. It hung by his side as if it were part of his flesh. 'I made a vow when I stood in this garden.'

The small piece of stone lay in his palm, heavy. One side was flat and smooth, glazed with tile of blue and white and green and even a colour like the orange fruit. The other side was jagged, rough-edged and broken, perhaps by a clumsy gardener.

The Queen's eyes widened. She snatched it from his palm and cradled it in hers. 'From the palace of my father,' she said blinking against tears.

He nodded.

'Look,' she said, waving it at Valerie. 'Alcázar!'

For a moment he thought she might hand it to Valerie, but then, she pulled back her hand, gripping the chunk of tiled stone so tightly, he feared he would not get it back.

Then, with a look of longing and a sigh, she put it again in his hand. 'You,' she said. 'You recall to my husband his duty. The throne.'

Suddenly, the stone seemed both cold and hot in his hand, as if her words had bewitched it. As he held it, he was, once again, standing in the palace, walking the tiled courtyards, feeling the sun on his face and hearing the splash of the fountains.

He closed his fingers around the sharp edges. 'He needs no reminder, Your Grace.' He looked at Valerie, then. 'Nor do I.'

It was his promise to her. He would take

her far from the horrible corner of England she had seen to the warmth and light of Castile. A far different place, where he could be a different man.

The Queen turned her gaze towards the window and looked out on the cool, blue sky of the May morning. 'I would smell again the *naranja* in the spring.'

How like Valerie she sounded, as if the plants and flowers held her to home. 'The orange blossoms, yes. And taste the fruit?'

She returned her hollow-eyed gaze to him. 'No. The fruit is bitter.' Her tone sounded void of hope, as if she knew she might die on this unfamiliar island, never to see her home again.

'You will see Castile again, Your Grace.' He looked at Valerie, gripped the stone and shoved it into his pouch. 'I swear by this stone.'

An unbreakable promise, to himself and to Valerie, who had taken this Queen, this country, as her own, even before she fully understood why he must leave England. She had studied the language, she had told the Queen of war plans, she had proved her commitment to Castile.

And yet, when he repeated his oath and

looked at the woman who would be his wife, he did not see the pride in her eyes he had expected.

He pondered it as he rode back to London, wondering all the way what expression he had seen on her face. He could not call her look that of determination, or even doubt.

Only as he reached the Savoy Palace did he understand the look he had seen in her eyes.

It was sorrow. When he spoke of Castile, he had seen only sorrow.

La Reina took to her childbed late on a summer day. Elyot and Katherine hovered the night long, along with Valerie and one of the Castilian ladies who knew enough of the language to be helpful. Between the two of them, they helped the midwife and the Queen to understand one another, as the Queen could not at once give birth and attempt a foreign tongue.

The Queen's younger sister, Isabel, was not to be found. Flirting with one of the guards, Valerie suspected.

La Reina had insisted that Valerie stay close and she suspected it was in part because the woman wanted a companion who knew as little of giving birth as she did. And so she

held Constanza's hand and wiped her brow
and when she was not translating from the
Queen's woman to the midwife, she muttered
sounds intended to be soothing, though she
could not have said what language she spoke.

Finally, the cry of a babe came as dawn
woke the sky.

The midwife, efficient, cleaned and swad-
dled the child. 'A healthy daughter.'

Valerie's empty womb tightened at the
words. Would she ever hold her own child?
One that Gil had fathered? She longed for that
now, more fiercely than ever before.

'Praise to God,' she murmured. A prayer
of thanks and petition.

Katherine smiled, with some of the sadness
of those statues of Our Lady, who somehow
knew what was to come. 'God would receive
more praise had she borne a son.'

Valerie sighed. Matters of state intruded
on even this most personal moment. Didn't
a daughter fill a mother's arms as fully as a
son?

Constanza, though a woman, had inherited
the throne in her own right and if there were
no sons, this child might do the same. Still,
the Castilian people wanted a king, a man of
their own blood.

And, a truth equally painful for Constanza *and* Katherine, a daughter meant that My Lord of Spain must return to his Queen's bed to try again for a son.

Katherine reached for the babe to take her to the nursery, but Constanza clutched the tiny infant to her bosom, shaking her head as if she, too, were no more than a child.

Then, she turned to Valerie and stretched out her arms. 'You.'

Valerie looked at Katherine.

'No!' The Queen's voice stronger than she had thought possible. 'You!'

Valerie held out her arms, uncertain, but somehow, the baby lay there as if in a cradle. The Queen smiled, at peace, and closed her eyes.

Valerie looked at the others, feeling help-less. 'What do I do now?'

The Queen let out a soft snore and Katherine reached for the small bundle. 'I can take her.'

Valerie hesitated. How painful for Katherine, to care for this babe of her lover's wife. And yet, even this a woman would do for love, to take care of a babe not her own for the sake of the child's father.

Katherine smiled and shrugged. 'It is all right.'

Yet the Queen had said *you*. She had selected Valerie, trusted her to take care of this most precious child. She hugged the warm, wiggling bundle close. Perhaps caring for this baby would convince God that she deserved a child of her own.

She smiled back at Katherine, but did not let go. 'I will learn. And I will not be alone with her care.'

Katherine took off her apron. 'Someone must tell John the news,' she said, not bothering to correct herself before Valerie. 'If you can care for the child, I will go.'

Valerie nodded and they embraced, laughing when the babe cried in protest.

Katherine paused at the door. 'Have you a message for Gil?'

'A message?' Did married couples communicate so? She and her first husband never had.

But she wished Gil could see her with a babe in her arms. If she could give him a child, maybe he would understand that even *his* home could be reborn. Maybe for a child, he would try to reclaim his own land instead of longing for Castile. 'Tell him I wait on his pleasure.'

Pleasure. She remembered his lips on hers, his arms around her. She had felt a moment's pleasure there, something she had never felt before. Some day soon he would be her husband, entitled to take his pleasure, whether she willed or no.

She looked down at the tiny face. Even if the act was as terrible as she remembered, it would be worth it for this reward.

Behind her the midwife sighed. 'If you are going to care for her, I must teach you a few things.'

Chapter Eleven

Word of the expedition's fate came early in July. Gil heard it first, as if on a bad wind in the dark.

The fleet destroyed. Men, burned alive on flaming ships, run aground at the entrance to La Rochelle's harbour.

To him fell the hated duty of delivering the news to Lancaster. 'My lord, the fleet, Pembroke…'

Lancaster looked up, all attention and smiles. 'What news?' Eager. Expecting to celebrate a victory.

Instead, defeat. And worse. 'Gone. All gone. The ships, the men, the money…' Words bitter and brutal. If Lancaster had seized the throne already, if the Castilians had not joined with the French, if…

Too late for wishes. Too late for prayers.

The man who would be King sat stunned, his face full of disbelief. 'We have never been defeated at sea.' The enormity of the disaster sank in slowly. And then, ramifications rippled across his face. 'And Pembroke?'

'Held for ransom by the Castilian pretender.' Worst of all insults. 'They are asking...' Gil said the number. A sum unfathomable.

'But he had twelve thousand pounds...' Enough money to keep the soldiers in the field for months. 'Surely that would be enough to set him free until the entire amount—'

'Gone.'

'Gone?' Another wave of shock. 'Where? How?'

He shook his head. 'In enemy hands. Or at the bottom of the sea.' Beyond their reach in either case. The money that was to pay the men, to buy victory in France, so they could move on to Castile, all lost.

Lancaster dropped his head, letting defeat roll over him.

Gil gripped his shoulder. 'We will avenge their deaths. The men are ready.' Near two thousand were gathering, ready to fight. 'When we take Castile—'

'We cannot land ships in France. How can we take Castile?'

The words a blow, yet he knew the truth of them. They could not reach Castile until they regained control of the sea. And so, once again, the dream of Castile, nearly within his grasp, floated from reach, as if washed out to sea and drowned with the English ships.

'We can,' Gil said. 'We will.' *Recall to my husband his duty.* The piece of stone from Alcázar hung heavy in Gil's pocket. The man must not lose hope. 'We have more ships. More men. We will land in Portugal.' That must be their path now. 'This is only a setback, like the blizzard in the Spanish mountains, which made the spring victory more sweet.'

Lancaster raised his head, shaken, still, but with a hint of his old energy. 'I must go to my father, my brother. We must plan...'

New plans. More battles. Lancaster, surely, must make the decisions now. His brother the Prince, once the most feared of commanders, could rally from his bed for only moments at a time. Not long enough to think or plan an invasion. And the King, by turns ill and distracted with his mistress, seemed distant, as if he were already contemplating the next world.

So would Lancaster's first duty be to a Castile they did not hold, to the lands in France they were losing, or to England itself?

'My lord. News.' The guard barely spoke the words before Lady Katherine followed him into the room.

'A babe, my lord.' Her words rushed, as if she had run the thirty miles from Hertford. 'Your wife has been delivered of a child.'

Lancaster's face lit with eager anticipation. 'A boy?'

A moment of anticipated joy. A male heir to the throne would give their cause new energy. It might even persuade more in Castile to support them.

'A girl,' she said, in a gentle tone, as if to soften the news. 'And she is healthy.'

'Congratulations,' Gil said, his voice a bit too hardy.

Not even a nod of acknowledgment from Lancaster. As if this second news had been more crippling than the first.

Gil did not move, uncertain how to comfort the man.

But Lady Katherine approached him without fear, laying a hand on his arm, putting her head close to his, in a posture too familiar for her to take with her lord and monarch. 'The Queen has named the girl María. After her mother.'

Her words roused him. And Gil again saw

steel in the Duke's eyes. 'The girl,' he said, 'shall be called Katherine.'

He heard a catch of surprise in the lady's voice. A slight flush of her cheek. Perhaps this was the reason the Queen had doubted her husband's devotion to duty. Did she think the man would prefer to stay in England, close to his mistress?

'You will tell the Queen of my decision,' Lancaster said, looking first her, then at Gil, before stepping back, putting the distance due a king between them.

The Lady Katherine inclined her head. 'I will so inform your lady.'

Silent, Gil looked from one to the other. There was more than lust in the Duke's eyes. He had thought the expression regret that the child was not the longed-for son. Perhaps it was more. Perhaps it was regret for a love his life did not allow.

'You have travelled far,' Lancaster said, his gaze still on Lady Katherine. 'But before you return to the Queen, take the news of the birth to my lord father.'

Gil struggled to keep the surprise from his face. The King could be expected to be generous to any messenger bringing him news of a grandchild. Far from being a burden, the chance to make such an announcement was a gift.

She murmured thanks, curtsied and turned for the door, then paused. 'The Lady Valerie sent a message for Sir Gil. She said to tell you she waits on your pleasure.'

All thought of war left his mind and he felt Valerie in his arms, her lips on his. It had all been too sudden. Her hesitation was understandable. Once they were wed and shared a bed...

'Gil. Were you listening?'

He blinked, as if the words had wakened him from a dream. He suddenly realised that the Lady Katherine had left the room and Lancaster had asked him a question.

'Forgive me, my lord.'

'We cannot count on landing any troops until we own the sea again.'

And once more, the invasion postponed. 'Then we will raise another fleet, my lord.' No hesitation. As if vessels could be summoned out of air. Now he was the one spinning impossible dreams. 'We will wipe them off the water. And then, we can land in Portugal, capture Castile, regain the French lands—'

Lancaster paused. 'On how many fronts can we fight?'

'As many as we must, my lord.' Brave words. Said as much to give himself hope as to answer Lancaster.

'If I had an army of men like you that would be true.' He shook his head, and was almost out of the door when Gil called to him.

'The Queen. She must be told of the…' He could not say defeat. 'Fleet.'

A puzzled look for a moment, as if the man had forgotten his wife.

Gil spoke again. 'Lady Katherine can tell her, when she—'

'No. She will be needed here.' His face changed, as if a new battle plan had occurred. 'You go. Tell the Queen the news. And tell her that her sister must meet us at Walling-ford next week.'

Had he been ordered to ride into battle, he would have grabbed the reins without hesitation. But this… 'Isabel?' He remembered lit-tle of the woman except a high-pitched titter which seemed to interrupt at awkward mo-ments. 'Why?'

'I would have her marry my brother Ed-mund. As soon as possible.'

Two daughters of a king marrying two sons of a king. Lancaster would be certain no question would arise of his family's claim to the throne.

He did not relish his role in delivering such an order to the Queen, or her sister, but he muttered his assent.

'And, Gil…when you return, bring the Lady Valerie with you.'

'Why?'

The Duke's face turned dark. 'It is time for you, too, to wed, so you can beget an heir before we leave. In case…'

In case. In case this expedition, too, ended in disaster.

In the days after the child's birth, Valerie had relinquished her hold on the child only to lay her in the arms of her wet nurse or her mother.

So when Gil was ushered into the room and saw her holding the babe, it took her a moment to understand the shock on his face.

A child. She was holding a child. As she might some day hold their own.

'There is an heir to the throne of Castile,' she said, quickly, lifting the child to show him. 'Her name is María.'

'My Lord of Spain wants…' The sentence

trailed away and he looked at her instead of the babe. 'You put off your widow's clothes.'

Heat touched her cheeks. 'As you asked.' He had noticed. And smiled. 'Does it please you?'

In truth, she loved the new gown. The design was simple, blue wool that followed her figure, with tippets that could be tied on to dangle, fashionably, from her sleeves when she was at court instead of acting the nursemaid. It made her feel young again and full of possibilities.

If she had hoped for words of praise, she was disappointed. But though he was silent, he smiled. And nodded. And his eyes seemed to speak of other things.

Of their kiss. Of what might come next.

She had put aside her widow's shroud, loosened the grip of the past, so when his eyes warmed to see her, she could smile in truth. When he kissed her again, maybe this time—

The baby fussed, breaking the silence.

And he was once again the King's man and not hers. 'I come with news. I must see the Queen.'

He did not need to say that the news was bad.

And so, still holding the child, Valerie led

him to the Queen's chambers and stood beside him as he told Constanza the worst.

The Castilian fleet, in partnership with the French, had destroyed the English ships.

A small expedition, Gil had called it, and yet the losses were enormous. Valerie could barely fathom it. Ships, men, money, all lost. And if the English ships provided no defence, would their enemies come here next?

Valerie risked the question. 'Should La Reina move to a place of greater safety?'

He shook his head. 'We think they look to Wales first.'

She explained via the translator that Wales was safely distant from Hertford. And, though she did not say it, from Florham.

In all this time, the Queen had made no sound.

Each word, translated and delayed, seemed to hit her like an arrow, yet she held herself erect, as if by sheer force of will. But regal as she was, Valerie saw the royal façade shaken, and had a glimpse of the woman as young as her eighteen years.

La Reina had expected, insisted, that they would return to Castile in months. Clear now, it could instead be long, painful years.

Without taking her eyes from Gil, Constanza reached for the babe and Valerie placed the child in the Queen's arms. Holding the infant seemed to steady her.

'*Qué son los planes corrientes de mi Señor, el Rey?*'

Then, in halting English. 'What does my lord the King plan now?'

As if the defeat were only temporary and there were endless money and men to throw into the sea.

Valerie knew little of men and war, but even she knew that men and ships could not be summoned from the air. But a queen could not admit that a thing might be impossible. A queen might demand the impossible be done.

Valerie glanced at Gil. His expression, grim, was touched with sadness, as if he mourned for the Queen, as well as for the men who had been lost. And she wished they were alone, so she could wrap her arms around him. So they might comfort each other.

'Your husband sent me to inform you of the news,' he said. 'He remains in London to make plans.'

'*Con nuestros fieles aliados los Ingléses.*' With our faithful allies, the English. Belittling them with a word, as if she were already on her throne and she alone could make or end an alliance.

As if Castilians instead of Englishmen would fight for her throne.

Her arms tightened about the child, who let out a squeak. Yes, from now on, all would be about this child and the children to come. Her duty to country and child, one and the same.

'England and Castile are joined, Your Grace,' Gil said. 'And in order to strengthen that connection, your lord the King has decided that your sister and his brother should also be married.'

The Queen blinked, silent. Such a decision, affecting her sister, and the succession, and yet, the King had made it alone. No, Constanza was not a queen in England.

'Isabel must travel to Wallingford as soon as possible,' Gil went on. 'The ceremony will take place in a week's time.'

Now Valerie spoke up in protest as words were translated. 'La Reina cannot travel so soon. She isn't even a fortnight away from the childbed.'

'My Lord of Spain knows that,' he replied. 'He understands that she will remain here.'

While the words were translated, Valerie

whispered to Gil, frowning. 'Is the wedding so urgent?'

'That, and other things. There is more…'

More? She looked at Constanza.

The words had just been understood and her face crumpled. Then, her regal expression returned. 'Isabel will be ready.'

'I will be here with you,' Valerie said, wanting to reassure her. 'We will pray for the success of the union and for Castile.'

'No,' Gil said. 'You will travel with Isabel.'

'Me? Why?' Blunt, angry on the Queen's behalf, she did not want to bow to his wishes.

But he was not looking at the Queen now. His eyes were on hers. 'Because we, too, are to be married next week.'

A shiver ran throughout her body. Fear or anticipation? She could no longer tell. Clear that even a queen had no life beyond what her husband would allow, yet despite it all, Valerie had a crazy surge of *want*, of desire so strong she could barely breathe.

'So soon?' And yet, she had known for months this moment would come.

'My Lord of Spain commands it.'

She turned away from him and faced the Queen again. '*Con el permiso de La Reina.* If she will allow me.'

A gesture, but all she had left to offer the Queen, whose husband had not given her the courtesy of asking whether she might spare the Lady Valerie at this time.

Constanza, straight and stiff, clutched the babe like a breastplate. Though she did not smile, she thanked Valerie with her eyes.

'Tienes mi permiso.' A nod of her head. Her dignity restored. Maintaining the illusion that she was, indeed, a queen.

They left the room, but when they were safely away, Gil took her arm. 'There is more unwelcome news for the Queen. Perhaps she should hear it from you.'

Gil had heard Lancaster charge Lady Katherine with the duty, but as he watched the Queen, and Valerie, he knew that would be too cruel a blow.

'What news?'

Her voice was steadier than he had expected. A testament to her courage.

'My Lord of Spain.' He was beginning to hate those words. 'He does not like the name chosen for the child.'

'Can he not allow the woman to honour her mother?' Then, she sighed, knowing the question's answer. 'What would he name the child?'

He paused. 'Katherine.'

Eyes wide, wordless, she clasped both hands before her heart. He met her gaze, both of them knowing the why of it.

'She did not ask for this,' Valerie whispered, intense.

'No. But he asked her to tell his wife of his choice.' Cruel, he had thought, even at the time. He was beginning to understand why a woman might prefer to remain a widow.

'Oh, no.' She covered her face with her hands, then raised her eyes to his again. 'Neither one should have to...'

And then he saw her realisation of why he had told her. 'You want me to do it.'

But seeing her pain, he changed his mind. 'No. I will be the one.' Though he knew not how he might frame the words.

She shook her head and wrapped her arms around him.

He enfolded her in turn, holding her against his heart, and he was not sure who comforted the other. She was warm and soft beside him and smelled vaguely of flowers, perhaps the roses she so loved.

You will be good to her, the Queen had insisted. And he had answered with certainty, not knowing that he could not protect her from every pain.

Not knowing that the worst wounds might be those unseen.

She raised her head. 'It will be kinder, if it comes from me. Better she not realise how many people know.'

As he had known of her husband's betrayal.

He nodded, beyond words now to praise her strength and her kindness. 'I must return to London. Come with Isabel as quickly as you can.'

She nodded. 'Katherine is not to blame. Nor is Constanza.'

He agreed, but held his tongue. Lancaster, the man he had admired above all others, should shoulder the most blame.

'Valerie.' He gripped her shoulders and looked into her eyes. 'I promise you. Our child will be called by whatever name you choose.'

She reached for his cheek, then stood on her toes to touch her lips to his.

As she turned away, he saw her wipe away a tear.

A few days later, Valerie came to take her leave, having asked to speak to the Queen alone. A private farewell, without the priest to report every word.

Or to witness the sorrow of the message she bore.

This, at least, she had done. Her Castilian, the Queen's English, the once-exiled pie bird, again allowed in the chamber. Somehow, they would understand one another.

La Reina still held her child. The babe had not left her arms since Gil arrived with the news of the defeat at sea. It seemed that the Queen would no longer trust any of English blood to care for her family. Nor her country.

Valerie sunk to a deep curtsy, strangely sad to leave the woman. They had found a connection, the two women, exiled.

'*Vaya con Dios*, Your Grace. I do not know when I will see you again.'

A trace of disappointment, quickly stifled, flickered across the Queen's face. 'An honour. The King, his sons, all to be there...'

And she would not.

No, it would be the Lady Katherine who would stand close to My Lord of Spain as Constanza's sister spoke the vows.

But she spoke no word of disappointment, nor of the hurried event that must have been her own wedding, on the run, in a strange country, to a strange man.

Never had Valerie understood her more.

'Yes, Your Grace,' Valerie said. 'King Edward himself, his son Edward, My Lord of Spain, they honour Castile with their presence.'

'You to help Isabel,' she whispered, in halting English. *'Preparar...'*

'I will do my best for her.'

Silence, then, 'Your Grace, there is something more. A message from Monseigneur d'Espagne.' Hoping she would not ask how Valerie came to have it.

'Más malas noticias?' As if any news he sent must be bad.

'He has decided that the child's name shall be Katherine.'

The Queen became very still.

Would she ask for an explanation? Would she refuse her husband's command? If so, what would happen then?

'I have no family with that name.'

'No, Your Grace.'

'Monseigneur d'Espagne? Has he...?'

She only wished he had. That would have made the tale more palatable. 'I do not believe so.'

A fierce frown creased Constanza's forehead. Perhaps she had made it worse by bringing the news herself. Perhaps it would have been easier for it to be public, official, re-moved from the private realm. Constanza must have wondered about Katherine and her husband, of course, but sometimes it was bet-ter to wonder than to be certain.

'María Catalina,' she said, after a long while. Then, she smiled. 'He may call her what he will.'

Valerie dipped in acknowledgment, hiding her own smile. The pie bird cackled, a sound suspiciously close to a laugh.

The Queen stroked her baby's head, but her eyes were still on Valerie. 'You are no longer *enlutada*.'

No longer in mourning.

It had been several weeks, yet the Queen had not mentioned it before. Did she disap-prove? Constanza herself still wore mourn-ing on most days, though her father had died three years ago.

Perhaps she mourned the death of her own life.

'My… Sir Gil asked that I do so.' At the memory of the kiss, and his hands in her hair, her cheeks flushed. Did the Queen see? 'I hope it does not displease you.'

There was sadness on her face, not anger. 'He wants to look on you,' she said. As her husband, obviously, did not. Then, a lift of the head. A royal smile. 'You will wed. Do your duty to your husband.' Then, a soft smile as she looked down at the babe. 'And your child.'

Valerie bowed her head. 'Pray God there will be one.'

'I to add my prayers.' The Queen shifted the baby in her lap, then lifted her heavy gold necklace with both hands and laid the chain across Valerie's hands. 'This to help.'

A gold cross, encrusted with rubies, dangled from the chain, weighing on her grip. Valerie looked at the Queen, eyes wide. 'Your Grace…' Words did not come. Such a thing was beyond her station. No doubt forbidden by the sumptuary laws. 'I cannot accept such a generous gift.'

'Yes. Honour marriage.' She reached out to stroke the swinging cross, as if to say farewell. 'La Virgen de Guadalupe. *Tierra*.'

Tierra. Earth.

Valerie looked at the cross. A precious relic from a holy place. A bit of dirt from her home. How Constanza must have clung to it, this piece of her homeland, as she clung now to the child.

'I am honoured.' Valerie lifted the piece and put it over her own head. The chain was heavy on her neck, much as the burden the Queen had put on her.

She gripped the cross, letting the edges dig into her palm. Sacrilege, to want a bit of the dirt of Kent to carry so, if she were exiled to Castile.

'Wear. Pray. For child. For Isabel. For Castile.' A whisper. 'For me.'

Valerie bowed her head, immediately doing as the Queen had asked. They would all, she suspected, need prayers.

Chapter Twelve

When Valerie arrived at Wallingford Castle on the Thames for the wedding, she saw Gil across the courtyard before he saw her.

Her pulse quickened, unexpectedly.

From this distance, she saw him as others might. Broad shouldered, confident, conveying both urgency and calm. A man others turned to for answers. One who was patient in providing them.

Something stirred, in her breasts, on her skin, delicate as a breeze or a ripple of water.

The thought of the marriage bed.

Was it possible that she might find the pleasure there some women did?

He saw her then, met her eyes and did not look away. Did she see a yearning in his or was that only her own hope?

She dropped her gaze.

Foolish dreamer. Be grateful if he does not beat you.

And yet...

The steward rushed forward, the servants swarmed and Isabel of Castile was helped from her horse and ushered into the castle.

Valerie wakened to her duty, pointing out which trunks belonged to the Queen's sister and which to her attendants until the final, small chest that was hers was the only one left and all the menials were gone.

She looked up to see Gil. His expression was stern, as she had come to expect, yet his gaze hinted at something more.

Our child will be called by whatever name you choose.

Scargill would never have said such a thing.

'Are you well?' he said awkwardly, as if she were a servant instead of his betrothed. As if the moments of closeness they had shared when alone had never happened.

She lifted her head. 'Very well, my lord.'

A frown.

'I mean, Gil.' His name still felt foreign. Too intimate.

Silent, he looked at her, as if assessing the truth of her assurance. Then he saw the

Queen's gift, weighing heavy on her neck. 'What is that?'

She lifted her hand to touch the cross as he reached to examine it and their fingers tangled, awkwardly.

He let go.

She smiled. 'A gift from La Reina in thanks for my service. So I could…' Pray for a child? Words too blunt. 'Earth from Castile. From the shrine of the Virgin at Guadalupe.'

'We will go there together to give thanks, when we reach Castile.' His expression lightened. 'Before St Crispin's Day, if all goes well.'

'So soon?' A flower did not change its colour with every new dawn. Yet war plans seemed to change between the rising of the sun and the moon. When he had spoken to the Queen, it seemed clear there would be no invasion this year. 'But the ships were lost, all was delayed.' Guilty, she realised she had rejoiced to think the defeat at La Rochelle had postponed the inevitable invasion.

But now there was joy in his smile, joy and excitement as she had never seen. 'King Edward will sail against the French, yes, but Portugal signed a treaty with us. We have an ally. Both expeditions can move.'

'But you had said the French, the Castilians, they might come to Wales.'

'We think to beat them first. All the men pledged to Lancaster have been called here to witness the wedding tomorrow. The next day, he will announce that we leave for Castile.'

To witness the wedding and then to fight for Castile. Poor, young Isabel. She was here not as a bride, but as a military rallying cry.

But Valerie, too, had been called here to become a bride. All thoughts of Constanza and Isabel and Katherine and Castile seemed to pale before that fact. 'So are we, too, to wed before then?'

'Yes.' His look of triumph and hope suddenly shifted and he looked at her, an edge of craving in his gaze, as if she were terrain to be taken. 'Tomorrow.'

Tomorrow.

No more hope to delay or postpone. And she had not realised, until that moment, how steadfastly she had resisted facing the truth about how her life would change.

She swallowed. 'At what hour tomorrow?' Each moment of freedom left to her, now to be counted, to be cherished.

'Immediately after Lady Isabel and Cambridge.'

She donned her smile, the one that meant nothing, and nodded. If Constanza could bear to be abandoned, if Katherine could bear to share her lover with his wife, then she could face marriage to this man.

'I will be ready,' she said, hoping her words disguised her fear.

But his words gave her strange hope, as well. He would leave soon, before there was time to know him, before there was time to do anything but give him her body. Like her first husband, he would to sail to war, leaving things as they were before.

'La Reina, in expectation of our wedding, has given me permission to leave her service, so that we may set up our household, at the Castle of the Weeping Winds.' So much work to be done there. Would she have time to lay out a garden? 'Until we leave for Castile, that is.'

The excitement on his face turned again to loathing. 'I told you. We will not go there again.'

'But…' She had thought that once he told her, once there was no more to hide, he would realise that he had a wife, there must be a home. A home in England.

She had, it seemed, been wrong.

But if she were not to go to Leicestershire, if she need not stay with the Queen, she might go home. To manage her own land. To tend her own garden.

Last time she had asked, he said it was not safe, but that was weeks ago, when they feared an invasion. Wales was on the westernmost side of the island. She would be more safe at home than at Hertford.

'In that case,' she began, struggling to keep the delight out of her voice, 'I shall return to Kent.'

Already, she could list all that must be done. Crops to tend before harvest. The ewes that were ready to breed. The quince tree would be showing its fruit, though they would not be ready for months. 'Until we must leave for Castile, I will—'

'You cannot.'

'Why not?' She had not thought this man as arbitrary as that, stubborn as he was about his past. 'You do not want me to return to Leicestershire and the Queen does not need me now.'

'The land is gone.'

'What?' Land could not disappear. 'That cannot be.'

'No longer yours. Lancaster has given it

to a banneret from Suffolk. He has already claimed it.'

'He cannot!' She could not breathe. It was as if her hand—no, more, her arm, had been cut off. 'The land was not Scargill's, it was mine, and *my* mother's and *hers* and more!'

'And you received your dower settlement for it.' His words sounded soothing and earnest. 'Lancaster has already transferred it to me.'

The land was dowered, which should have meant it was hers, inviolable, hers and her family's unto all the generations to come.

But things had changed, since the time of Queen Eleanor and the first Edward. A woman's dowry was what she brought to the marriage, as well as what she could take from it. Some husbands preferred the flexibility of coin, the value of the land that could be spent even while the land itself remained. If her mother had made such an arrangement for her, the Duke would be well within his rights to give the dowry to her husband in cash.

To him, to both of them, the land was no more than a chess piece, to be moved, traded, exchanged for a more important or convenient piece of property that suited Lancaster's purposes.

'But the settlement will be protected,' Gil said, thinking to reassure her. 'It will be yours if…' A pause before he spoke the words bravely. 'If anything happens to me.'

And she saw, so clearly, that he did not understand. A man who hated his own land could not understand how much she loved hers.

'But the man who holds it now, there are things he should know.' Who was this banneret? Was he worthy of what had been entrusted to him? 'I must tell him about the crops, about the flowers…'

About her dear quince tree, with fruit beginning to grow, and the pink-and-white roses, probably past cutting now…

Gil placed a hand on her shoulder. 'You have a steward. He can tell the man everything he needs to know.'

She closed her eyes against the tears. It was not the steward who had measured the angle of the sun in order to be sure the tree would have the best light. He had not been the one to prune the roses, nor to select where the pink ones were to be set and where the white.

She gripped the gold cross, with its scrap of Castilian soil, the only earth now truly hers. Then, she raised her eyes to his. 'And what of my things?' A mirror. A comb. The cloaks she would need come winter.

Now, his expression softened, as if he suddenly realised something of what had been snatched away. 'They will be packed and sent.'

'Sent where?' Now, she had no home.

A moment of confusion, as if he had not thought of the question. As if all he needed was what he could carry into battle. 'Is there a lot?'

She thought of the things that were hers, not part of Florham, and shook her head. 'But there were a few tools for the garden. A spade. A trowel...' Things worn to the shape of her hand.

'When we are settled in Castile, you will not need to do that work. We will have gardeners.' This was said with boastful pride. As if it were a gift, this magical future, this castle in the air of Castile.

Instead she felt as if she was to be pulled from the earth, ripped up like a plant that might or might not be suited for the soil of its next home.

She looked down at her cross, filled with dirt from a place she had never seen. What was the soil like? Parched or moist? Loam or sand?

'You have what you need in your trunk now, yes?'

Silent, she nodded.

'When the wedding is done,' he continued, 'you will return to the Queen until we regain Castile. Your things will be packed and sent to you there.'

She sighed. The Queen would no doubt understand.

He called over one of the men to lift her trunk and gave him directions. 'He will show you where to sleep,' Gil said. 'The castle is crowded. You will have to share a room with the other ladies tonight. And tomorrow...'

His words brought heat to her cheeks.

Tomorrow, after the wedding, she would be sharing a bed. With him.

As Valerie watched the English King and his sons gather to celebrate the wedding of yet another son to yet another daughter of Castile, Valerie felt the ache of La Reina's absence.

Or, perhaps, she concentrated on the other wedding to avoid thinking too deeply of her own.

The soon-to-be husband, Edmund of Langley, Earl of Cambridge, brooded in the corner, glumly sipping his wine. This marriage would bring him neither money nor power nor even the illusion of position, unless Constanza and his brother and their offspring all departed this earth.

Meanwhile, La Reina's sister Isabel was all smiles and laughter. Flirting with men not her husband, batting her eyes and pursing her lips as if to kiss, under the guise of trying to speak the English tongue, she floated through the Hall, giggling and laughing. It was as if Constanza, only a year older, had assumed all the responsibilities of a parent and a queen, leaving her sister to act the child.

Isabel was only two years younger than she was, but Valerie felt infinitely older and wiser than this bride, for Valerie, at least, knew what awaited on the other side of the altar.

At least, she knew what lay behind her in her first marriage. Now, once again, she would be given to a man, tied to him through eternity.

Would she have two husbands in Heaven? A question only the theologians could answer.

But she knew what marriage on earth meant. And still, she hoped.

As they watched the exchange of vows, her eyes strayed to Gil, standing beside her. Shoulders strong enough to wield sword and shield. Lips that too seldom smiled. Fighting his past and living for the future.

This man had shown her kindness, made her think thoughts near as foolish as she had the first time, when she thought a husband would be a helpmeet instead of a scourge.

This man was not like the other, true. A stern warrior, yet Gil had the smooth courtesies of the nobility and even some inborn kindness, though that could be no more than the care one took of a horse or a hound. Certainly he did not understand her yearning to stay in England, attached to her own earth.

The ceremony concluded. The guests moved towards the Hall, ready for a banquet, and she stood, awkwardly, next to her husband-to-be.

Finally, the chapel was nearly empty and they walked, together, to stand before the altar, where the priest, Lady Katherine and Lancaster waited. Katherine stood safely distant from her lover, but the angle at which she held her head, the softness in his smile, the light in their eyes when they exchanged glances…she could see it all.

And more, she could see Gil watch them, with an envy that mirrored her own. The sort of love they shared? No man, or woman, should expect that within a marriage. Gil, as most men, would find it elsewhere.

She must expect that, even encourage it from the beginning, so that he would feel free to find it with another.

With kindness and a child, she would be content.

And now, they stood before the priest, in an empty chapel, for this afterthought of a wedding, arranged for the Duke's convenience. An honour, to have him as a witness. Gil must be proud.

Lady Katherine moved to Valerie's side and squeezed her hand, a quick encouragement. But they could not linger over this ceremony. Celebrations for the royal couple had begun in the Hall and they waited for Castile's King to welcome his brother into the royal family.

It was the height of summer, yet her fingers were numb with cold in Gil's large, warm hand. Now would come the words, the words which, once spoken, could never be undone. *I plight thee my troth.*

The priest began to speak.

Gil reached for his bride's hand, so small, so cold. It chilled his palm. Did she fear him so much?

Or was she simply disappointed?

Each time he spoke to her, she bowed her head and acquiesced to anything he wanted, but today, he had seen her struggle when she realised he had no home to offer her. Nothing except the promise of Castile.

The priest muttered the final words.

Gil dropped her hand.

Lancaster clasped him on the shoulder. The Lady Katherine embraced Valerie. In all that time, his wife never raised her eyes to his.

They hurried into the Hall, where the feast of celebration for the royal wedding had begun. Few noticed them. A handful of the men who knew him gave him congratulations and said a kind word to Valerie. The newly married royal couple, sitting at the high table, was the centre of attention this night.

Isabel was twirling a silver cup between her fingers, mimicking the grotesque faces of the figures carved on it.

He and Valerie stood beside each other, awkwardly looking out over the room. And all he could think of was that he would come to her bed tonight. At last.

'The lady over there wearing red. Is she not lovely?'

He glanced in the direction Valerie was

looking and nodded, without attention. 'I suppose.'

'Fair haired,' she continued. 'A pleasing laugh. A pleasant woman to be around, don't you think?'

'I do not think of her at all,' he said.

'Or Lady Johanna, there. I hear that she sings and plays most delightfully. You might enjoy that.'

'What?' He had heard men say that women were confusing creatures, but he had never spent enough time with them to know, except for the Lady Cecily, who had always been a woman of logic and duty, except when she was not. 'Why are you pointing out any of these women to me? We were just wed.'

'But that does not mean...' She stumbled on the words. 'I know you see other women, that sometimes...'

What was she talking about? 'If a woman is before my eyes, I will notice her, of course.' As one might appreciate a finely turned sword or a well-made wine from Bordeaux.

Her cheeks turned red, but she did not turn her eyes away. 'I know you will do more than notice.'

He grabbed her arm then, steered her to a quiet corner, away from the crowd, and studied her face. He could see not a hint of jealousy. 'Do you expect me to take a leman?'

'Many men do.' So calm. He had sensed more passion when she spoke of her quince tree.

Well, no doubt she did expect it. Her husband, now Lancaster…

But he was not either of them. 'You will be my wife, Valerie. I do not need a concubine as well.'

'But what if—?' She bit her lip.

'What if what?' It would take all the energy and wits he could muster to manage life with *this* woman. Whatever would he do with two?

'If I am not…if you are…'

'If I am tempted?' There seemed to be something more in her question, but he could not understand it. 'If I have the time and energy to be tempted by a woman not my wife, which I cannot envision, I will go to confession and practise my penance. Now, will you be content?'

Strangely, given the look on her face, she was not. He sighed. He could barely juggle his duties to God, England, Lancaster and now marriage. He certainly did not need an additional complication.

But she had already known a man. Maybe

she was the one... 'And you?' The very idea was as painful as a wound. Already possessive of her. Already he cared too much. 'Are you tempted by another man?'

But her astonished look of surprise said it clearly. No, more than surprise. Disbelief.

She lifted her chin and looked him in the eye. 'I am not!'

'Good,' he said sharply before he thought.

It would be his job to make certain she never would be. And he was beginning to look forward to it.

Valerie did not know how it had been done, but in a castle overflowing with guests, she and Gil had been given a room to themselves.

As the evening wore on, she slipped away from the feast alone, asking a serving girl to take her to the room they would share. Her husband—strange to use that word again—had left her side at last to join the men, drinking to future glories. She had angered him with her awkward attempt to interest him in another woman. He would come to her when he willed, if he came at all.

As she climbed the stairs, the echo of wine-filled laughter faded behind her. After she dismissed the serving girl, she lay naked beneath the sheets, staring up at the wooden ceiling, unsure if he would come to her this night at all.

Light still lingered and, as she watched it wane, she thought of the ways she should have prepared.

I could have perfumed myself. Put powder on my cheeks. Used sage and salt to sweeten my mouth...

Dear God, do not let me fail again.

She knew what must come. It was the wedding night. The man would have what was his right. With her first husband, that had never been a pleasant experience.

And yet, Gil's kiss had been different...

The unfamiliar spark of desire fluttered within her again, *there*, between her legs, the place that must accept him. Was this what some women felt for their lovers? Could it be that way with a husband?

Could it be that way with *her* husband?

Tempted by another man? No. But by Gil? Tempted, indeed.

Yet when the door opened, every muscle clenched in protest. She had not realised, until that moment, how much fear her body carried. Fear stronger and more powerful than her hope.

'Valerie? Are you ill?'

The light had dimmed. She could not see his face clearly, but he did not sound irritated, as Scargill always had when interrupted from his own amusements. Still, his last words to her had been sharp ones. She could not know his mood.

She sat up, keeping the bedclothes before her. 'Forgive me. Gil.' She must remember to say it. 'I did not think anyone would miss me.'

'Of course I would miss you.' Said without the annoyance she had expected. 'You are my wife.'

'Had I known you needed me beside you, I would have stayed. Next time I will ask your permission first.'

The vows complete. Once again, she must remember to obey her husband, to understand his wishes in all things.

And tonight? She must appease him, entice him to bed, cajole and please him, start the marriage by slaking his lust or things would go badly from this point on.

Just as they had before.

Keeping the sheets over her nakedness, she threw back the covers on his side of the bed, making room for him. And yet, even covered, her breasts seemed to sense his nearness, to ache for him to come closer…

She shifted her bare shoulders, uncomfortable, waiting, aware of his eyes looking at her naked arms. One hand clutched the sheet before her, the other, clenched against what was to come, was hidden in her lap.

Her body at war with itself, wanting, fearing, waiting.

Instead, he looked away, moving towards the window, not the bed. 'I will not lie with you tonight.'

'But we are wed.' She tried to remember the calendar of church days for abstinence. Was this one that even married people must avoid? Then, another thought seized her. 'Is it because I am a widow?' Did he not want the leavings of another man? Yet he had known that from the first.

He looked at her, puzzled, and then smiled. 'You will not be the only woman I have lain with who knew another man.'

A moment's relief. She had even wondered whether he might be untested.

But still, he did not approach the bed.

She must have made him more angry than she knew.

Or, perhaps, he was only tired. If so, it was

not her place to force him to his duty. The day
had been long, the wine plentiful. Perhaps he
was in a mood to rest. 'If you want to sleep…'
She shrugged and shifted to the other side of
the bed. 'You need only wake me when you
are ready.'

'Why are you like this?' he said, abruptly.
The softness had left his voice.

'Like what?'

'Pretending you have no opinions, no desires of your own.'

What a strange man she had been given. 'I
am your wife. Your wishes are now my own.'

And yet he did not smile to hear it. 'But
still, you have wants, needs, hopes, opinions.
Lady Cecily, Queen Constanza, even Lady
Katherine let their thoughts be known.'

Women with more power than she would
ever know.

She did not know what to make of him.
Was this some kind of test? 'And my earnest
wish is to be a good wife to you. To bear the
son you want.'

'Are you certain?'

She had thought Gil to be a stern man with
a soft side and some pain of his own. She had
never thought him witless. 'Of course I am.'

He approached the bed, pulled a stool

closer, and sat. 'No. I mean do you truly understand and agree? My son, our son, will carry the blood of the Brewens, even though he does not carry the name.'

'You told me, yes.' A confession over and done. Why would he belabour it tonight?

'And I asked if you wanted to be relieved of the burden of this betrothal. You did not.'

She remembered the conversation, vaguely, but so unused to being allowed to have an opinion, let alone make a decision about her own life, it had never occurred to her that he might be serious. 'No. I did not.' No woman refused a marriage ordered for her by the son of the King.

'But although we are wed, bearing such a child is not a decision to be made lightly.'

As if bearing a child was a decision of any kind. She almost laughed. She could barely say how much she wanted a child. If she had been given a choice, she would have chosen yes, long, long ago. She wanted, needed a child. Her land, the land she thought would always be hers, was gone. Without a child, what would be left to her if she again became a widow? She wanted a child so badly that she would not have objected to a babe with horns and a tail.

But his expression was serious, as if the very thought was a burden he was carrying. And he sat, hands clasped, elbows on knees, looking as if he might be praying. Waiting to hear her answer.

Astonished, she simply looked at him for a moment. What sort of marriage might this be?

This man could be stern and angry, but then, the disgrace of his family weighed on him still, as if he doubted whether he was enough, just as he was.

That, she could understand.

She laid her hands on top of his. 'I do not make the decision lightly. I am willing to be a dutiful wife, to carry your name and, God willing, your child.'

His duty given. And hers. She expected nothing more than that.

And yet, she wanted to give him comfort. And his eyes spoke of something beyond obligation.

He reached for her shoulder, but instead of pushing her down on to the bed, he let his forefinger glide across her collar bone, drift over her shoulder, and float down her inner arm.

'Marriage can be more,' he whispered, covering her hand with his, 'than duty.'

She pulled her hand away. 'Can it?'

She wanted no more than duty. As his wife she would attend to him, meet all his needs and demands, but to care for him with her heart, not just her hands? To truly mourn the loss of love, when he found another?

That, she could not bear.

'Yes.' He wrapped his arms around her, pulled her to him and pressed his lips to the bare skin at the curve of her shoulder. 'I have seen it.'

'In truth?' She barely knew what she spoke, only that words were safer than his touch. And yet she felt it building, that desire he wanted, that desire she thought she could never feel.

'Yes.' His lips moved against her throat now. 'Between a man and his wife.'

Ah, what a chivalrous fool she had for a husband. For a moment, she wondered, even wished she could give him what he wanted.

She could not.

She wanted no such passion with her husband. Nor with any man.

So as he lit a candle and tossed aside his tunic and shoes, she lay on the bed, ready for him to pull the sheet away until she was bare to his gaze and to the night air.

And she squeezed her eyes shut, ready to submit to whatever he wanted, wise enough to expect nothing beyond than duty and telling herself she would be content with that.

And knowing she lied.

Chapter Thirteen

Gil forced himself to go slowly.

He wanted her to think of no other man, of no other world than the one he would build for them. So he took long, slow moments to caress her skin with his fingers, with his lips.

But he had waited so long, wondering what lay beneath her mourning weeds, that it was hard to hold back.

He had thought to discover her gradually, the curve of her shoulder, the delicate arch of her back, the colour of her skin untouched by the sun. But she had bared herself already, though still hiding behind the sheet, so that if he wanted, he had only to reach and he could take all of her. More temptation than a man could resist, especially on his wedding night.

But he tried.

Concentrating on her pleasure helped him

subdue his own. He let his fingers explore her skin, every inch of it, as if it were the terrain of battle. Not to wage war, but to wage love, to know where a light touch might please and where it might tickle.

She lay with her back to him, too enticing otherwise, while he trailed his fingers lightly across her skin, from her shoulders down her arms, across her wrists, on to her palms, and then his fingers stroking hers and moving on. One side. The other. Alert to any change in her breath, to any involuntary movement, hoping for a shudder of anticipation, a moan of pleasure, for anything that would prove she enjoyed his touch.

Instead, she lay, bare and unmoving beneath his hands. Relaxed? Tired? He could not say.

So he started again. Pulling the sheet down to bare her to the waist, pushing her dark hair to the side, then kneading the tight muscles of her shoulders before beginning with a light descent again, down the back of her neck, down her spine, wanting to let his fingers slip between her legs…

She tensed.

He stopped.

Too soon? He did not know what this

woman wanted. It could take nights, weeks, to learn what might give her pleasure. Perhaps she was a woman who would be roused by a kiss.

He touched her shoulder, whispering for her to turn. And then, as she rolled on to her back, everything he had dreamed to see, everything that had been hidden was open to him.

The candlelight glowed across the pale skin of her breasts, small and perfectly formed as he had dreamed. Below the curve of her waist, her hips flared, wide enough to carry their children with ease. And between her legs, a thicket of dark curls, both concealing and beckoning.

He widened his eyes, taking in the vision of her, uncertain where to begin. Uncertain he could hold back. Below the waist, his skin, still imprisoned in linen and wool, was crying out to meet hers, but he was reluctant to let her go so that he could pull off the braies and wrestle with the hose.

It was her pleasure he wanted first, so he held back his own desire. Stretching out beside her, he let his hand roam again, from the tip of her chin, down to the tip of one breast, the place, finally, that brought a gasp to her lips. As if without thought, she offered them to him more fully.

His lips, soft, but hungry, followed his fingers across her skin. He touched his lips softly to her shoulders, to the base of her throat. Not a kiss. Something much more delicate. A promise.

Her breathing quickened. And his.

But before he claimed her lips, he stopped and leaned on an elbow, to study her face. Her eyes were closed, not in languid desire, but squeezed shut, tightly.

'Valerie, open your eyes.'

Obedient, she did, but without meeting his.

'Valerie, look at me.'

Dark eyes unfathomable. Was she ready? Had he kindled her desire? But he could no longer hold back. Pulling her to him, he took her lips, desire in his kiss. Her lips, taking, then giving to his. Yes. Now. Hesitation forgotten, he rolled on top of her, reaching to part her legs, expecting to find her ready…

She stiffened and her hands met his shoulders, as if to push him away.

Dazed, he paused, unsure what was happening.

He moved, struggling to open his eyes, passion and frustration muddling his brain. She had said she did not fear him. So how could her passion change to resistance?

He raised his hands to Heaven. 'What's wrong?' The words, not spoken gently.

And when he looked down at her, she was curled inward, hands covering her head, as if to avoid his fist.

'What's wrong?' he had shouted.

And Valerie had braced for the blow. For a hailstorm of words and a punch, a slap, even a kick.

Instead, silence.

'Valerie?'

She opened her eyes, realising where she was and whom she was with. Not Scargill. Not any more.

She sat up, pulling the sheet before her. She must make this right, reassure him, please and pleasure him again. A man expected no less, especially on his wedding night.

'Nothing.' Said quickly, eagerly, with an adoring gaze. 'I did not mean…please, forgive me.' In the darkening room, it was difficult to read his face. Did she see a flash of irritation, or was it confusion, in his eyes?

He stood, stepping away from the bed, but still watching her, as if studying her long

enough would allow him to see all she kept
hidden.

'Was it that bad?' he said, finally. 'With him?'

'What? No. What do you mean?'

'You are not a good liar.'

But she had been, once. Scargill had never
known the difference. Or perhaps he had not
cared.

She sighed and braved his eyes. 'I don't
know what you think I am lying about.'

'Every time I have touched you, you have
flinched. And just now, you looked as if you
thought I was going to hit you. I can only assume that your time with your husband was
unpleasant.'

'No more than most.'

'Why do you say that?'

Because my mother told me so. She shrugged.

'Did he hurt you?'

She blinked against the tears. 'He was my
husband.' There was no more to say. That
meant he had the right to do whatever he
pleased and she, no right to gainsay him.

Gil sank on to the stool by the bed, so he no
longer towered above her. 'I am your husband,
but I am not the same man he was.'

She had thought, hoped, that was true, but
her body's memories were strong.

He took her hands in his and squeezed them. 'I would have you take joy in our joining.'

'God does not want us to join unless we mean for children, so it should not be pleasant.' Not for a woman. Men, she had noticed, always seemed to take pleasure in the act.

But then, men did not bear the children.

'All women do not feel as you do.'

She was beginning to learn that. From the way that Katherine looked at John, she suspected they both took great joy in each other. 'I will do my best to be a good wife to you.'

He dropped her hands. 'With gritted teeth?' There was an angry edge to his voice.

Now she must undo the damage. Her previous husband had been so, from time to time. Coming home with a frown. Stomping about the room. But once he had slaked his lust with her body, calmer. Even with a smile for her.

She wondered whether he had been the same with the woman whose silk he had carried.

She stretched out her hand. 'Forgive me.' Her fault. Always. That was the way to begin. 'That is not the way I meant it. Just because something is a duty does not make it unpleasant.'

'Valerie, don't lie to me. Not any more.'

She swallowed, afraid she might choke on her words. 'I do not lie to you.'

'You just did. With those words.'

'Why is it wrong to please you? To say what you want to hear?' The question sounded more desperate than she had hoped. 'That is the way of the world.'

'That is what is wrong with it!' The words exploded and set him to pacing the room. 'The King says he is still the greatest warrior in Europe. The Duke says he is King of Castile. And I say we will reach Seville by Yuletide.' A sad, self-aware smile. 'When I come home to my own bed, I want to sleep in truth.'

'But aren't there times when all you want is a willing wife?' *Or one you believe to be so.*

He creased his brow, as if considering her words. 'When I do, I will say so.'

She considered saying that now he was the one who lied, but she did not.

What a strange marriage she had fallen into. She had thought she could do as she had done before. Give him her body, as one would throw a bone to a dog to keep him busy, and keep her thoughts her own. He wanted both. And more.

'And if you are not willing,' he said, when the silence had grown long, 'will you tell me?'

Yes—that was her first thought. But that was a lie so she did not speak it. 'I don't know. I have not been expected to be, to do, as you ask before. Have you been so honest with all your women?'

'I have not had so many,' he said. 'And I have not had a wife.'

'Ah, well, a wife is different from other women.'

A wife, she thought, must be the keeper of the lies. Her husband's and her own.

Gil stood, deliberately far enough that he could not reach her. Any closer and he might do as she expected, simply grab and take her.

He *did* want a willing wife, but what had happened to the ferocious woman who refused the scarf he had offered? That was a woman who might make a partnership of their union, not this meek and humble impostor who thought of marriage as an exchange of bodies as mercenary as Constanza and Lancaster's. He wanted to give her, and himself, something more than that.

And still she gazed at him with an adoring, and utterly false, smile. 'It is my duty to be anything you want me to be.'

Duty. As if it were a shield to ward off whatever he said. Well, he had lifted duty. He knew the heft of it. 'I want you to come to me with desire, not just duty.'

He moved closer and put his hands on her bare shoulders, her flesh fire on his palms.

She gasped. Let the bedclothes slip…

Her breasts, small and white and tempting, again bare to his gaze, rising and falling quickly, as if she, too, were having trouble catching her breath. She did not lower her eyes this time, but met his, as if taking his measure.

Or was she simply trying to be the woman he wanted her to be?

Yet he could not subdue his body's response. The weapon between his legs, ready for her, straight and hard, sent heat through his veins, crowding words from his brain. His hands roamed, gently, across her chest. The buds of her breasts springing to life.

Yes. This.

She *was* his wife. She was willing. He must be gentle with her. Then, she would believe…

He leaned to kiss the curve of her neck,

feeling the flutter of her pulse. Her desire, kindled. He was sure of it. If she could forget Scargill, if she could learn to trust him...

Stroking her arm, her back, gently, slowly. Then, he sat beside her, softly, so she would not be startled, and put his arm behind her, tucking her close to his chest. She had closed her eyes, let her head drop closer to his shoulder. The sheets covered her lap, her arm across them as if to hold them in place, but her breasts, pale in the dark room, were open to his fingers, his lips.

A sound from her throat. No words.

And he wished he had learned one of the love poems to murmur in his lady's ear.

The bedclothes were tangled between them, still hiding her below the waist, but he let them be. Before he could take her beyond duty to desire, he must lull her into comfort.

And then, she reached for him. Arms around his neck, fingers in his hair. Surely a kiss now...

He took her lips. Pressed himself against her as if they could join from the kiss alone, felt her lips, eager, and then...

She went slack in his arms, eyes squeezed shut, arms out, as if offering herself as a sacrifice to some vengeful heathen god.

If he took her now, no matter how outwardly willing she seemed to lie beneath him, no matter how gentle he tried to be, they would never be able to start again. This would be what she expected of him. And of herself.

Now he was the one to go slack.

He tore himself away, struggling to breathe like a normal man, trying to keep his voice steady, so she would not fear he was angry.

He was. But not with her.

Adultery, it seemed, was the least of Scargill's sins.

He rose and stepped away. 'I will not touch you tonight, my wife.' Perhaps he could make sense of it in the morning. 'Let us sleep.'

She moved to the far side of the bed. He hesitated, unsure whether he could safely lie beside her, but he lay on top of the bed, his back to her, trying to keep a safe distance.

Tired as he was, sleep did not come.

Nothing will change, he had promised her. Promised something he knew nothing of and could not, truly, fulfil. They were married now. Everything had changed. He was just beginning to discover how.

But he had also discovered, to his sorrow, that the one thing he wanted, wished desper-

ately *would* change seemed to stubbornly remain the same.

Her fear.

Valerie lay awake, stiff, hands clenched,
forcing even breaths so that he would think
her asleep. Would he touch her even so? Would
he reach for her in the night, only half-awake,
with no words, only growls and grunts, then
pound against her until he was satisfied?

That was the way it had been before.

Or perhaps he would touch her gently
again, coaxing her body into feelings she had
never realised she could have.

If not tonight, it would be tomorrow, or
some night yet to come. And she would submit. Because she must, must, bear a child
from this marriage.

She had never expected anything more.
And yet, when he pressed her tonight, probed
for her feelings, he had almost made her see
his dreams of chivalric love.

Now she was acting the fool. In the poems
of chivalry, the man and woman in love were
never married, or at least, not to each other.

Even if it were possible, even if there were
couples whose marriage went beyond duty,

she did not want such passion in her life, in her bed.

For she would lose him. To war, capture, death. Even if he lived, even if the passion he wanted flared, it would not last. And when, like Scargill, he tired of her, the pain of watching him love another woman would be even worse.

What do you want?

Easier to say what she did not want.

She did not want to mourn when she lost him.

The sun woke him, the light coming through his closed eyes.

Gil sat up, head and stomach still woozy from the night before. His wife, strange to use that word, stirred beside him, but did not wake.

Or did not want him to think she did.

He slipped out of bed and pulled on his tunic, not looking at her again.

Morning had come and still, he had wanted to take her with more than his body. Wanted it in so many ways that he could not name them. But in between his dreams, he had made a decision.

He would not touch her again. Not until she wanted him as well.

He heard the rustle of the bedclothes and turned to see her sitting up, watching him.

He had faced men wielding a sword, close enough to kill him, but faced with her eyes, her steady gaze, he was, for a moment, struck dumb.

The sheet slipped, exposing the side of her breast. 'Would you come to me this morning, husband?'

At her question, his resolve was shaken, his body screaming *yes*. 'No. Not now. Not like this.'

Was she disappointed or relieved? He could not say and hated that he did not know.

The false smile he had come to despise. 'Tonight, then. Or when you will.'

He took the risk, then, of leaning closer to her. 'Not today, or tonight, or any time at all until you can tell me in truth that you want me in your bed.'

She blinked.

Was there desperation when she faced him? 'When, then? And how? Am I so hateful to look on?'

'No!' He was doing this all wrong.

'Do you not wish to enjoy the pleasures allowed us? Even the church says that coupling to create children is no sin. Can we not…?'

He pulled her to him. 'We can.' What a dullard he was. No good with women. He had little to offer right now beyond his seed. Did she think he would not even give her that? 'But not like this.'

'If we do not lie together, our marriage is not valid.'

'Then you can have it annulled and be the free woman you wanted to be.' Even he could see her pain at that idea. What man would think to wed her then? But wasn't that what she had wanted?

She pulled away. 'You said you wanted me to speak truth. You know that without…consummation, we have no hope for the child that we both want.'

Blunt words. He counted the days. Perhaps four weeks, no more than six until he sailed. Time enough to get her with child. Just not time enough to know whether he had succeeded.

'Not now, not yet, not until…' Until what? What perfection was he waiting for? Hers? His?

'But we have no time!' She gripped his hands, tightly enough to bruise. 'Tonight. A few nights. Then you will be gone and, unless we share a bed, there will be no son!'

The son he had told her he wanted above all things. But he wanted something more now. A woman who loved him. Not for his protection or because he could give her a child. One who loved him for himself. Even if he was a Brewen.

'Then there will be no son.' He pulled himself away and stood. 'The King will announce my expedition to Castile this morning. We must gather in the Hall. Dress, and come quickly.'

And he left the room, not waiting to hear her protest.

Chapter Fourteen

Then there will be no son.

Silent as if he had slapped her, Valerie stared at the closed door. Nothing left. Nothing she could do.

No son.

No protection. Nothing.

She had tried all that she knew, tried to bend herself to his will and she had, again, failed. Again, she could be left alone and helpless, with no child to protect her from being handed to the next man of the King's choosing.

What could she do now? Only try, again, to please him. And pray she would succeed.

As Gil descended the stairs, he met Lancaster, who greeted him with a smile and a slap on the shoulder. 'Late abed with your bride, I see.'

Said with a grin. As if he knew what happened in a man's marriage bed.

Well, he need not know what happened in mine. 'Yes, my lord.' An attempt to laugh. He hoped it sounded sincere.

'And did she like the gift you chose for her?'

Gift.

Too late he remembered the beautiful cup the Queen had disdained and the plaything that Isabel had twirled last night. These were things a wife should expect from her husband.

'Gift?' He cleared his throat. 'I have not thought of it.' No surprise, then, that she would not welcome him with loving looks. He had done nothing to woo her, not even presenting her with a token of their union.

'You must give her something.' Lancaster frowned. 'Perhaps in my possessions...'

'No!' Words well meaning, but insulting to his pride. 'The responsibility is mine.'

The Duke nodded, his mind on things to come. 'We gather within the hour. My father will speak.'

'We will be there,' he said, wondering that King Edward would be the one to proclaim their expedition instead of My Lord of Spain. He had no time to ponder why. His mind should be on what he might say to the men, as soon as he heard the words.

Castile! And Sir Gilbert will lead us to victory!

Instead, he was thinking of a way to remedy his failings as a husband.

A carved cup, a jewelled brooch, a necklace to rival her gift from the Queen—those things took time he did not have. What could he give her today? This week? Before he sailed with the fleet?

Nothing more than a promise.

'Husband?' Above him on the stairs, she paused. Properly garbed as his wife, her hair was again hidden beneath a veil, visible to no man but him. The power of possession and responsibility shook him. She was his now. Her future, her happiness, all in his hands.

Hands all but empty.

Alcázar's stone weighed heavy in his pocket. Castile. Castile must be his gift.

'Come,' he said, as she joined him. 'We have a few minutes before we must be in the Hall.'

He led her outside, no time to find a proper time or place, to a shaded corner of the courtyard, where she stood, expectantly, waiting for him to speak.

He reached into his pouch and gripped the stone, its jagged edges painful on his palm. 'As your husband, I would give you a wedding gift.'

'Gift?' There was surprise on her face. Had she not thought he knew enough to give her a token? Well, he had done nothing to make her think otherwise.

He pulled the stone from his pouch, but as he did, it broke in two.

He cupped both hands together, trying to save the pieces, and when he opened them, one rested in each palm. He lifted one hand, so she would take a broken half. 'I promise you our future.'

She lifted the broken piece and stared at the white, blue, orange and green pattern. 'Your stone,' she whispered. 'From the garden at Alcázar.'

'Where we will start again. Together.'

For she, as much as he, needed to leave the past behind and start afresh.

She stared at the rock in her hand, not looking up. A broken stone, disappointing, no doubt.

He folded her fingers over the coloured tile. 'Hold this piece. The other will come with me to Castile. When I reach the palace, I will

send for you and they will be reunited. I shall
pursue this unto death, even as I would strive
to reach Heaven.'

He kissed her, gently, to seal his pledge.
And when he broke the kiss and looked at
her again, her eyes, large and dark, seemed
to promise a future without end.

She looked down at the stone in her hand
and back at him. 'I have nothing to give you.'

'A son,' he said. After he gave her Castile,
surely then... 'When you are ready, you will
give me a son.'

Gil led her back into the Hall as she slipped
the stone into the pouch hanging from her
girdle.

The time had come for the King's proclamation, anointing Gil as commander so that
he could realise the promise of the stone.

Flanked by his two sons, Edward and John,
the King stood at the front of the Hall. Even
from a distance, Gil could see the King had
aged, his energy faded. He must be saving
what was left for war. And his mistress.

A herald called for quiet.

King Edward stood to speak. He and his
sons would sail within a month in the largest
fleet ever seen. No one, not the French nor
the Castilians, alone or together, would dare

threaten England's ships or shores again. England would be master of the sea once more.

A roar filled the hall. Edward had not led men into battle himself for years. His very presence promised victory.

And yet, Gil felt a sense of unease. He knew the difficulties of finding so many ships. And the King had said nothing of the expedition to Castile.

But when Lancaster rose, Gil stifled a smile. It must be left for My Lord of Spain to speak of Castile.

Gil knew he should wait until he heard his name spoken aloud, but he could not stop the pride that lifted his courage and swelled his chest.

'Today,' My Lord of Spain began, 'I call on all those pledged to me to follow my father, to report to Sandwich in a month's time for service at sea.'

At sea.

The fleet he had gathered to take them to Spain would be at the King's command.

At sea. There would be no invasion.

No Castilla.

Gil did not move, no longer certain that he breathed.

As the men raised their voices to pledge

their allegiance, Valerie whispered in his ear, 'How can Monseigneur d'Espagne reach his throne if he stays at sea?'

'He cannot,' he said, surprised he could speak so calmly. His heart, his mind, his tongue, cleaved one from the other, yet each could still work.

He had been promised he would be at the King's right hand. He'd thought that meant his counsel would be honoured. All of it had been an illusion. His plans, Lancaster's...at the end King Edward alone ruled their course.

'Will you go to Castile after that?'

He shook his head. 'No.' A month's time. They would sail in August, already later than hoped. Soon would come the autumn winds, then winter, no season for war. 'Not this year.'

She clutched the Queen's gold cross, as if clinging to the ground it held. 'When will you go?'

Her question seemed an accusation. Already, the promise he had made impossible to keep. 'Perhaps in the spring.' Words of hope. He no longer knew Lancaster's mind.

'I was angry,' she said softly, as all around them, men cheered at the challenge to come, 'that La Reina was not invited to witness the marriage of her sister.' Then, she looked back

at him, sadness in her eyes. 'Now, I thank
God she is spared the knowledge of this betrayal for a few days longer.'

Remind them of their duty, the Queen had
told him. She had seen, more clearly than he.

Later that morning, after the toasts had
been given, the decision irrevocable, Lancaster was ready to ride to the hunt, leaving
lesser men scrambling to change the plans,
move the ships to new ports and ready the
men the King had commanded.

Lancaster had asked Gil to join him. It
was to be a celebration, an escape before the
rigours of war. But Gil had no heart for it now.

'Wait here,' he told Valerie and approached
his lord, as men and horses milled in the
courtyard, wondering what words to use. He
would fight as commanded, of course. But
beyond that...? 'My lord, I will meet you on
the coast. I must...'

What must he do? Mourn. He must mourn
in peace.

Understanding mixed with longing on Lancaster's face. 'My father...needed me. Castile
must wait.' His hand rested on the saddle, as
if eager to mount his horse and leave. 'I promise you. Our time will come.'

Gil was sick of promises. But he nodded, as if he believed. 'Someone should take word to the Queen.' This, he thought, this he could do. For Valerie and for himself.

'Yes. If you would. And take Lady Katherine back to Hertford. I would be grateful.'

Still numb, Gil nodded. It would take only a few days. Then what would he do in the weeks before they sailed? 'I will see you on the coast.'

Lancaster mounted, then paused before he rode on. 'When you come to the coast, bring Lady Katherine with you. I would see…my children before I sail.' Looking down from his perch on the horse, the man was quiet for a moment. 'Where do you go now? Home?'

Gil had no home and nowhere to go except to a wife he had already disappointed.

And he had nothing to offer her except a broken stone.

Wait here, her husband had commanded.

And so Valerie waited, as the room emptied until only the echoes of the men's cheers remained. Cups had been raised to the success of the coming expedition and they did not seem to care where they went, or who they fought.

And after her husband raised his cup, he did not look at her again.

Hoofbeats now, as the hunters rode out of the gate. Gil came back inside, grim and silent, looking as if he had lost his way.

She approached him softly, as if trying not to wake him. 'You do not go to the hunt?'

He shook his head. 'We must take this news to the Queen, you and I.'

We. Wed now. One being.

'La Reina will be...' Valerie searched for a word. 'Disappointed' was much too mild. 'Sorrowful.' A queen, but still at the mercy of her husband.

He nodded. 'She will need comfort.'

And she saw the sorrow in his own eyes, sorrow that meant he understood the Queen's.

His kindness seized her heart. It was not Constanza's husband who would try to give her solace and ease her pain. It was hers. And she was so proud of him, for he had shown more care for the Queen than the woman's own husband.

And now, he looked at her, grabbed her hand. 'And, Valerie, what I promised, still, that has not changed. It is my pledge to you. Our future.'

Valerie looked down and murmured something like assent, afraid that he might see the truth if she met his eyes. The blow of losing Castile was his, Constanza's, Lancaster's. He would not see shared sorrow in her eyes. He would see relief.

Unto death, he had promised, thinking that would please her. Thinking she, too, longed for a palace in the sun. Hand in her pocket, she gripped the piece of stone he had given her. His promise of a future she did not want, a shining grail always just beyond his reach.

He knew, despite all she had tried, that her body did not want to join with his. But he did not know that she did not want to join her life to the life he wanted.

She shivered. No, she could never tell him not to go. Never tell him how much she wanted to stay here on English soil, even if it meant living in the crumbling place that had been his family's.

He said he wanted the truth. But he did not want that one.

No. Kind as he might be, he would not want to know that she hoped never to see Castile.

They did not rush to Hertford.

Valerie, Katherine, Gil, a few retainers, had travelled largely in silence through the

Rumours at Court

green countryside. Valerie devoured it with her eyes, thankful for the reprieve. She had gained one more winter, perhaps one more summer, before she might be forced to leave.

When they arrived and joined the Queen, the sky was pink with sunset, the pie bird was chattering, and the Queen received them, holding her baby, looking like a statue of the Madonna and child.

Valerie and Gil dipped their greetings and let her know that Lady Katherine had gone directly to the children.

Easier for both women.

Then silence. The interpreter looked at them, then at the Queen, waiting.

Valerie glanced at Gil. They had not spoken of what to say, of how to tell her. The wedding, perhaps. Begin with happiness. 'Your sister is married, Your Grace. The celebration was worthy of her rank.'

The Queen looked up, expectant. 'Her husband, what kind of man is he?'

Valerie hesitated. If sisters could be so different, so could brothers. And this one, she suspected, was not the man Lancaster was. 'I saw him only from afar, Your Grace.'

'A fine commander,' Gil added, too quickly. From the sound of his voice, she knew he said it only to please the Queen. For a man insistent on truth, he could dance on the edge of it, when he chose. When he, too, hoped to set a mind at ease.

'My sister. Is she happy?'

What a strange question. As if a woman could expect happiness in a marriage.

'She seemed so, Your Grace.' Isabel's laughter still rang in her ears. Not for her the sombre days of duty to country and to God.

'And you, too.' She looked from Valerie to Gil and back. 'You are married.'

Gil glanced at her and took her hand. 'We are, Your Grace.'

She could not stop a smile. Unfeigned.

'But there is other news, Your Grace.' Gil again, dropping her hand and braving what must be said. 'News I regret to bring you.'

'No Castilla.'

Not waiting to be told. As if she knew. As if she knew she had been lied to from the first.

'Not this year, Your Grace. The threat at sea must be answered. We cannot risk a landing on our shores. The ships that destroyed ours last month…'

And she listened with half an ear as Gil made excuses for the King, for her husband, for their loyal English allies, for all who had

failed in their promises to this lonely woman.
But he tried, swearing again, as he had to her,
that La Reina would see Alcázar again.

A promise given to comfort the Queen, for
it was not his to make. This much Valerie
had learned. A woman must answer her husband's wishes, but a man lived at the mercy
of his lord.

'And is there more? Do you bring a message?' the Queen said, finally. 'For me?'

Valerie looked at Gil. No one had thought
to send personal words to Constanza. Not her
sister or her priest, and certainly not her husband.

At their expressions, the Queen nodded,
without surprise, and let her gaze travel
around the castle walls, walls which had become her prison, not her home.

Valerie understood her longing and she
wished, fiercely, that she had the power to
take this woman home, even though it meant
Valerie would then be the one trapped in exile.

Would she have the strength to make a
home in that foreign place? For Gil's sake?

But the Queen had neither her husband nor
her country. Only her child was left to her.
Only the babe she could not even call by its
right name.

Gil tried to explain. The decision was made quickly. My Lord of Spain and King Edward, but La Reina shook her head, as if tired of lies.

'Go,' she told him. 'I would speak to your wife.'

Even the interpreter was dismissed, a signal that they would speak in their own, cobbled language. The Queen, no longer able to maintain her strong façade, handed the babe to Valerie, so as not to let her tears stain the child.

For a while, the two of them sat, not speaking, letting the pie bird's chatter fill the silence. Gradually, the tears stopped.

'Your *madre*,' the Queen said, as the baby slept in Valerie's arms. 'Did she have *amor* with your father?'

Love? Valerie doubted that any of her mother's three marriages had included love. 'My mother never spoke of love. Only of a wife's duty.'

The Queen looked towards the window, which faced south, as if she might see as far as home from there. 'My father loved my mother. Very much.'

An insight she had not expected. How much more painful, then, her own marriage.

'It is an unusual thing in a marriage, I think.'

The Queen turned to look at her with deep, sad eyes. 'They were not married.'

Valerie swallowed, unsure what to say. In love, but not married. Did the Queen know how this mirrored her own life? It was hard to say. She did not like Katherine, but Valerie had never known whether the Queen knew, in fact, of her relationship with the Duke. The Queen had been isolated from the court rumours, certainly. 'Did he have...other children?'

She had almost said *legitimate* children.

'No. They forced him to marry other women, once, twice. But he did not give them *niños*. Only to my mother.' Such pride in her words. As if children could only be born of love.

They both knew the lie of that.

'So he made you his heir.' An illegitimate daughter named a king's successor. Something England would never see.

'Yes. And after she died, the Archbishop declared they had been married.'

Valerie's eyes widened. Was such a thing even possible? 'According to God's laws?'

And Constanza, who she thought had

loved God above all things, simply shrugged.
'Sometimes, love is stronger.'

'You have seen such a love, Your Grace. I
have not. It is hard for me to understand such
a thing.' Harder to believe it.

'Your husband, does he love you?'

A strange and terrible question. 'I believe
he wants to. He wants that for us.'

'And do you love him?'

A simple question. And the answer different from what it would have been a few days
ago. 'I might be able to.'

She wanted to, in a way she could not have
imagined before she'd met Gil.

'You will go with him now.' A command.
'To your new home.'

But there was no home. He refused to go to
his. Hers had been taken away. Where *could*
they go? 'I believe he expects me to continue
to serve Your Grace and I am happy to do so.'

They shared a smile, but the Queen shook
her head. 'It is right that you cling to him.'

'I will try, Your Grace.' This Queen had
chosen duty and been denied love. Perhaps
she wanted others to find it.

The Queen stretched out her arms, ready
to hold the babe again, and Valerie handed

the bundle back, her arms feeling strangely light and cold.

'And also,' the Queen said, in a tone that signalled a new subject, 'I have Castile's heir now. The other children of the King, not heirs, should live elsewhere. With Lady Katherine.'

And so. She does know.

How painful to be forced to atone for her mother's sin. Now *she* was the married Queen, watching her husband love another woman, just as her own father had once done.

If she saw the similarity, she did not say. But she also knew what it could mean. At least she now had a child. And if Katherine, too, had children by Lancaster?

Well, those children, at least, would not be in line for her throne.

Valerie's heart hurt for them both. The woman who loved another woman's husband. And the wife who must watch her do it.

'As you wish, of course, Your Grace. I am certain it could be arranged.' Lancaster, too, would no doubt prefer dropping the pretence that Katherine served the Queen. It would make it easier for them to be together.

'You tell her. Tell her what I want.'

'I will, Your Grace. You need not see her again.'

The reassurance seemed to bring a moment of peace. Even a smile. Then, the Queen waved her hand. 'You may go.'

Surprised, she bent her head, then touched her necklace. 'Thank you. For this kindness. And for the necklace. And for so many other things. *Vaya con Dios.*'

She had feared a stern, unhappy face, but instead saw understanding. 'You with him, after. Tell him. *Te lo permito.*' Permission. From one who could have commanded.

'I hope so, Your Grace.'

The Queen's brow was furrowed again. 'To make a child. You must make a child.'

Her cheeks flamed. 'Yes, Your Grace.'

That, if not Castile, was a goal she and her husband could share.

Chapter Fifteen

Valerie whispered only a few words to Gil of what the Queen had requested, but by his expression, she could tell that he, too, understood all.

'Lancaster asked me,' he said, 'to bring Katherine to the coast to see him before he sails.'

'I will tell her,' she said. 'And until then?'

'We will take her wherever she wants to go.'

And after that? Valerie could not guess what would happen.

She found Katherine in her chamber, eyes closed, head back, as if she had fallen asleep, but she opened her eyes immediately when Valerie came into the room.

'I come…the Queen has asked…'

Katherine sat up. 'What is it? What is wrong?'

Valerie sat beside her and took her hand.

'The Queen thinks it would be better if you, if the Duke's children from his first marriage, had a separate household.'

A sigh. A smile. Relief. 'Yes, I see.' She seemed almost giddy with it. 'I will speak to John, I mean, My Lord of Spain. He will arrange things. He will know where the children should go.'

John. The Duke. The King.

Valerie squeezed her hand. 'Katherine. She knows.'

The happy smile on her face shattered like a broken mirror. She looked away.

'I said nothing to her.' Surely Katherine would not think she had told her secret. 'I swear.'

Katherine shook her head, resigned. 'She knew before you did.'

You, the Queen had said when the babe was born, insisting Valerie, not Katherine, hold her. All the times the Queen had insisted that Valerie serve her instead of Katherine took on new meaning.

'A wife always knows,' Katherine said.

Yes, just as she had.

'Gil will take you wherever you want to go. And when the time comes, he will bring

you to the coast so you can see…' No need
to say more.

Katherine's face spoke her gladness. 'I will
go to London now. A few of the men can accompany me. Gil need not come himself.'

'What will you do in London?'

'I will settle the children into their new
household and make sure all will be taken
care of without me.'

'I thought you would stay with them.'

She shook her head. 'After John sails, I will
go home. To Kettlethorpe. I should leave court
before…' she touched her belly '…it becomes
too clear.'

A child. Sired by My Lord of Spain. And
she seemed to delight in it.

Valerie embraced her, feeling as if every
woman in the world had earned God's favour
except for her. 'But will you, what if…?' She
did not know how to ask. To bear the man's
child, out of wedlock. 'Does the Queen…?

Did the Queen know this, too?

'I don't know. She may recognise the signs.'
Now, it was Katherine who seemed to comfort her. 'Do not worry. I will be well. And
you…' Her tone changed. She took Valerie's
shoulders and squeezed them. 'Your time will
come. You will be happy in your marriage.'

A wistfulness in the words. As if she envied Valerie her marriage, just as Valerie had wished herself a widow, as independent as Katherine.

She looked towards the door, to be sure they were well alone, then she gripped Katherine's fingers. 'Katherine...' Could she even confess the truth? Yet she could bear the isolation no longer. 'He will not sleep with me.'

Katherine's look of puzzlement matched Valerie's own. 'But you are his wife. Surely he does not think you still mourn.'

She shook her head. 'I have told him I am willing to do my duty, but I think he wants more. Something like you and...' Embarrassed, she stopped.

'Something like John and I have?'

Valerie nodded. 'Something I have never seen in a marriage.'

'And what do you want?'

Did she want love? Did she even believe it possible? 'A son.'

Katherine studied her, waiting a moment for her to say more.

'I want, I must be with child before he leaves, in case...'

In case he does not come back.

She let the words drift away at the expression on Katherine's face. That moment of pain…she must have been thinking of the Duke and what might happen if he did not return.

'I have made it clear that I am willing.' But when he did touch her, her body remembered only the fear. 'He wants more than willing. He wants eager.'

'You can be that. You can coax him into your bed.'

'Did you…?' Then she bit her tongue. She could not accuse Katherine of seducing Lancaster.

But Katherine knew the question. 'I wish it had been so simple. Sometimes, it cannot be denied.'

'That's what Gil wants.' Something that could not be denied. Was she brave enough to risk that? And if she did, could she love him enough to embrace the life he wanted in a foreign land? 'We have so little time. And I don't even know where we will go for the next few weeks.'

He had not said. Only to come here. And then?

She was weary of the unceasing movement. It was the way of the court, she had learned. London to Hertford. Leicestershire to Wallingford. She wanted familiar earth beneath her feet.

She missed her garden. Missed the dirt between her fingers. Missed seeing the plants change, gradually, day by day, as a child might grow. You had to look carefully to see the changes, but they were there.

But that was no longer hers. Even Gil's beloved Castile did not belong to him. There was only one place they could go now. The one place he did not want to go.

'Home.' Strange to call his castle by that name. 'We will go home.'

She did not know how she would persuade him. But she must.

Gil mounted the stairs to the top of the castle walls, leaving the women to talk. Who knew what women spoke about? They seemed to know things in some mysterious way. The Queen had learned that Lady Katherine and her husband were lovers. No one had told her it was so, yet she knew what he had not recognised when it was right before his eyes.

Because he had not wanted to acknowledge it. Because in this way too, Lancaster, My Lord of Spain, had failed him.

He pulled the Castilian stone from his

pouch. Pieces of the blue tile had fallen away. The white tile was scratched. All as broken and battered as his dreams. He weighed it in his hand and looked down at the river. If he hurled it forcefully enough, could he hit the water?

Soft footprints on the stairs. He pocketed the stone and then Valerie was beside him again. They stood next to each other and looked out on the river, and somehow, he felt a moment's peace.

'Katherine will go to London,' she said, finally, 'until it is time to leave for the coast. You and I do not need to go with her.'

He nodded. And let the silence stand.

'She carries Lancaster's child.'

He let a curse slip.

His wife raised her brows. 'Lady Katherine rejoices.'

'But he...' How could he explain? The Duke of Lancaster, example of all the things a knight should be, had loved his first wife beyond all reason. Gil had wanted a marriage like that. Lancaster had made him believe it was possible. But now...? 'It is shameful.'

'You expect much.'

He did. 'The love he bore his first wife, even the poet wrote of it.'

'Most men are not so faithful.' And yet, her voice carried a wisp of hope.

He knew, now, why she could not believe. That was the worst wound Scargill had left. The one Gil was not certain he could heal.

'I will be.' A promise, unlike the last, that he alone could fulfil.

'I did not ask that of you.'

'I ask it of myself.' As he had all his life, striving for perfection.

'No man is perfect.'

How well he knew that, now.

'You said,' she began softly, 'that I must truly want you in my bed, before you would come again.'

His pulse quickened. 'Yes.' An arrogant demand, thinking about it now. 'Are you saying that you do?'

A shy smile, proof that he had been right. 'Yes. Let us begin anew.' And now, a long, slow look from her, assessing. 'At home. At the Castle of the Weeping Winds.'

Valerie saw him stiffen, resisting the suggestion, but she did not break her gaze.

'You cannot leave the Queen.' His first excuse.

'She has given her permission. The Queen,

of all people, understands the importance of an heir.'

He flushed at the word and she could see the very thought had sparked desire. But still, he fought the idea. 'It is five days' ride. We would have less than two weeks before we would have to return to London.'

'Then we must not delay.'

He smiled, then, as if he knew she had caught him.

She was beginning to understand, now, who he was and why. Of course, he would want more than obligation from a wife. He deserved more. She only hoped she could give it to him.

Her hand on his arm, near a caress. 'You asked for truth. The truth is, I do not know if I can give you all you ask. But I want to try.'

You can coax him into your bed, Katherine had assured her.

She moved closer now, lifting her lips, not certain he would take them. Now she was the one to risk, giving what he might again reject because it did not come with feelings that he deemed worthy.

Chin higher. Eyes closed. Waiting.

The July sun warmed her face, while his arms took her, loosely, without force.

And then, a kiss.

Gentle, this one. Starting over. She would begin again as well, forbidding memories to intrude. This man's scent, his skin, the taste of his kiss, these were still new. She quieted her mind, stilling the emotions he had asked for, and tried to allow her body to feel what it might.

And it felt…right.

She let herself sink into him. Strength and power in his kiss, now, but not force. And she could actually return the kiss, return the passion, fooling him into thinking it might be the love he wanted.

Or was it herself she fooled?

This time, the kiss ended gradually, lovingly, and she sighed when his lips left hers.

'We shall leave,' he said, his words unsteady, 'tomorrow.'

They travelled more quickly than Gil had expected. Only a few retainers rode with them. The rest had taken Katherine to London, but being always with others, they said nothing to each other that could not be said before all.

And they did not touch each other again.

He had sent a messenger ahead, but the

steward had had little time to prepare for their
arrival. Still, when he introduced Valerie as
his wife, he could see that the man understood
that things would be different.

At least, Gil hoped so.

But within the walls of his childhood, the
past surrounded him anew. As if nothing had
changed. Or could.

As night crept upon them, he was awkward next to her, uncertain what should be
done. There had been a wedding night, such
as it was, in which they had barely touched.
The nights on the road there had been no
demands, no expectations. But tonight, she
had made it clear, they would share a bed
in full.

'Give me some time to prepare,' she whispered. 'And come to me, when the moon
rises.'

Restless, unable to think of anything but
his wife, he wandered the halls, seeing with
fresh eyes the ruin the castle had become.
Why had she wanted to come here? Why had
he agreed?

But when Gil entered the sleeping chamber
that night, it resembled nothing he remembered.

Candles, wine, soft scents. He looked

around, feeling as if he had stumbled into someone else's quarters.

Suddenly, gentle hands, touching his back. A goblet of red wine pressed into his palms. And Valerie, soft and close. She had put off her veil and her gown and stood clothed only in her linen chemise, delicate enough to reveal the tips of her breasts. 'Welcome, my husband.'

First, she had stiffened in his arms and pushed him away. Then, she had lain unresponsive beneath him. And though they had shared a kiss, more, since that time, here was a woman he did not recognise. She was acting like the veriest paid companion. And his body was reacting.

He took a sip of the wine and studied her face, trying to understand her. Her solicitude was welcome. Too welcome. And why should he not succumb to his wife's allure? They had agreed between them.

And yet, something was wrong.

He put down the goblet. She leaned against him, breasts pressing his chest. Desire, hot and sharp, quickened. Weariness fled. Was it his wife he wanted, or just a woman? His body, less particular than his heart, might not be clear on the difference.

She tilted her head back, lips parted, reaching for his.

Even as she stood on her toes, she was shorter than he. He dipped his head, met her lips and lost himself in her.

Was this the same woman who had slept beside him, untouched, in their marriage bed? Now, she was eager.

So was he.

His lips pressed to hers, then breaking to brush her cheek, her ears. To murmur her name like a prayer.

Awkward in her response, and yet she continued to kiss him, matching him kiss for kiss. Her body pressed his, chest to loins, where he was stiff and ready. She did not speak, not in words, but her breath quickened, signalling she, too, was excited.

He had demanded love, as if it could be commanded, but even if she felt only lust, well, tonight, that would be enough.

He could not think beyond that now.

She pulled him towards the bed and he stumbled, finally opening his eyes again to look at her. She was panting, still, but the look on her face was grim. Determined. He thought she had changed, and yet… He stopped and let go of her hand. 'What are you doing, Valerie?'

She looked over her shoulder. 'Why do you stop? I promised to try. Is this not as you asked?'

Yes, his body was screaming. He could barely think beyond his desire. But he did not want to take her like this.

He shook his head, not trusting speech, and motioned to the mattress. 'Sit.'

Obedient, still, she did. And he wrestled with his breath and lowered himself on to a bench, safely out of reach.

'When I told you we were to marry,' he began, 'I said nothing would change. I was wrong.'

Her smile, genuine. 'You could not know. You had not been married.'

'You are kind.' He had been a saddle-goose and she had every right to say so. 'It is clear that marriage changes everything. One of the things it has changed is you.'

'Me?' Her smile disappeared.

'You said a wife is different. What did you mean?' He should have asked before, the night she said it. Admittedly, he had not cared so much what a woman thought before. Another thing that had changed.

He was trying to learn her expressions so that he could know when she spoke truth, when she lied and when she simply concealed. At the question, her eyes had widened and he glimpsed the woman who had faced him that first day.

She had an answer, it seemed. She was simply trying to decide whether to tell him. 'The truth,' he said. 'Tell me the truth.'

'Very well.' She spoke in a slow and measured tone that suggested she was speaking it. 'When I was a widow, I could act on my own. Once we married, we became one person.'

He was a man of war, not of law, so he knew only vaguely what the law thought of a widow instead of a wife. 'Of course. Husband and wife are one.'

'And the one is *you*. I ceased to be.'

He rubbed his head. Would this make sense if he had not taken a sip of wine? 'You speak in riddles. Here you are before me. You walk, talk, breathe. You have a soul.'

'Yes, but I now need your permission to do…anything.'

Had he ever denied her? If so, there had been no malice in it. 'None of us are entirely free to follow our own devices.'

And then, a moment's memory. *We cannot ask Sir Gilbert's promise before he has the chance to speak to his wife.* And yet he had not thought of doing so, so certain that a wife's wishes would be the same as his own.

'What do you want to do,' he asked, 'that you cannot do now?'

She studied him before she answered and there, finally, was the look he had feared. The one that pitied him for his lack of understanding. 'I will never know, now.'

And then, a thought. Worse. What if it were not that he prevented her from doing something? What if it were something he was forcing her to do?

'You said you would try, Valerie.' He moved the bench closer and took her hands in his. 'I am tired of paying penance for Scargill's sins. Do you understand, truly, that I am not the man he was?'

Then the tears came. Ones she did not even try to stop. 'Yes.'

'Do you know because I've told you or do you truly believe it?'

'I want to believe. But it is my mind that knows. My body...'

Her body knew no other way to respond to a man.

He moved to the bed and gathered her close, stroking her hair and letting her sit and cry without interruption. Finally, when the tears were spent, he raised her chin and looked at her. 'I will not hurt you. I promise.'

And she smiled, as a mother might smile at a child who promised he only wanted one last sweet. 'No. You won't.'

And he realised, with those words, that he would not hurt her not because he was a better man than Scargill, but because she had developed her own armour and she would never let any man hurt her again.

Did she love him? Or was she only submitting to him, as she would to any man that had been named to wed her? Did he still want to know? 'Let me try to teach your body something new.'

He said nothing, then, but with his kiss.

A kiss, two, more, lips that explored her face, ears, throat, skin, kisses without counting. Without ceasing.

Scargill had never bothered with kisses.

No. I will not think of him. I will not think at all.

For to think was to stiffen with fear, then to force herself to acceptance. Not this time. Gil wanted, deserved, better.

He lifted her in his arms, still kissing her,

gently, as if knowing that the power and strength of his desire had triggered her fear before and was determined, this time, to put her feelings before his own.

Braver, now, she let herself feel. That had worked before, for a time. Eyes shut, she felt his lips, then his fingers, soft, gentle, and aimless as a feather. There was no rush. No goal. Instead of racing to mount her, he meandered, no end in mind but to discover what she hid and what she liked.

This time, kisses were not power, not urgency, though she knew they could be. And now, in his arms, there was nothing to do, nothing to fear. Loose, comfortable as if she were in sleep.

And yet…excited. In a way she had never imagined possible.

He trailed his fingers over her bare arms, then over the sheer linen so that the tips of her breasts rose to meet him, aching for more. He left her shift, her defence, in place, but then brought his hand up her bare leg. A touch still so soft that it might have been the air instead of his fingers that caressed her.

Was the moon high? Did the wind howl? Again, she could not guess. Content, more than content, to lie in his arms.

His fingers glided over her knee and up her thigh, pulling her shift high and exposing her fully to his gaze. But only that. He made no move to mount her. His fingers, his lips, stayed a safe distance and then paused. Waiting. Temptingly close.

She opened her eyes.

To see his smile. The one she had too seldom seen. The one that promised...everything.

'You are so beautiful.'

Words no man had ever said to her before. And yet she believed him.

She lifted her arm, trailed her fingers across his shoulder and down to his elbow, the hair softer than she expected. At her touch, he, too, seemed to need to catch his breath, making her smile.

And then, she slipped her hand on to his back, pulled him to her and met his lips.

She could feel the weight of him, the hardness of his shaft through the fabric, pressing her leg, and still his lips and fingers, moving, as if he would touch every inch of her skin. Yet he did not take more than she offered. Her kiss, her arms...

Her body moved of its own now, her legs parting, opening to him, an invitation...

He paused. Pushed himself away and

waited, until she opened her eyes again, and looked at him.

'Will you trust me?' he asked.

And she could do no more than nod.

Instead of mounting her, he ducked his head, parted her legs, and then the lips that had touched her everywhere kissed her there.

And, oh, what she could feel. In the past, she had blocked the pain, but that had blocked her pleasure, too. This, *this* was the desire that made women risk all. She had no more sense of anything but him, her, their bodies connected. It was as if she had taken wings, like an angel, no longer bound to earth.

Blasphemous thought. And blasphemous to care more for pleasure than duty. But this was beyond pleasure. This was—

And then, she could not think at all, but burst into a thousand, thousand pieces, that mingled with his, until there were no longer two of them, but only one.

Finally, much later, when she had come again to earth, she opened her eyes to see her husband leaning over her, smiling.

Now, she knew the joy that smile promised.

'And so,' he said, his voice husky, 'you can believe.'

Now, she could smile in return. 'And so, my husband, let us make a son.'

The joy in his face as he took her to him again was beyond words, but not beyond flesh.

And so, open to him as she had never been to another man, she let herself forget that she had not told him every truth.

What do you want to do that you cannot do now?

I want to stay in England. I do not share your dream of Castile.

That secret she still kept.

Only later, when the dawn touched their bed, did she worry that perhaps she no longer could. For she had been able to lie to others, who did not know her lies from truth, nor cared to know.

But this man cared. And this man, more and more, could tell the difference.

Chapter Sixteen

$\mathcal{V}$alerie had hoped, in bringing him back, to show Gil that he could be content in this place, to make it home enough for him to release his dreams of Castile. So the next afternoon, she persuaded him to walk with her, thinking that he would love the feel of his earth beneath his feet as she did.

In the weeks since their last visit, summer had come in full. Green leaves and grass bright enough to hurt the eyes surrounded them. She saw little pasture land. Oxen, but no cattle.

And nothing cultivated for beauty alone.

No one had loved this earth for a long time. What was grown, poorly, as far as she could tell, was nothing more than basic necessities. Near the kitchen, a few herbs thrived, against all odds, in the neglected garden. Everywhere, she saw work that should be done.

'We can meet with the steward, Husband, before you leave, to discuss management of the land during the time you are gone.' She had more than one idea of what must be done, but though she was the lord's wife, she was newly come. She would have to have his support, his permission, before the steward would listen to her.

'I have never done so before.'

She shrugged. 'And this is the result.' She regretted the words immediately. Criticism would not convince him to give his home the care it needed. 'While you are away, I can make certain the plans are carried out.'

'This is not a place you will live. Ever.' No spark of interest, still. 'The Queen awaits your return.'

'No, she...' She had not told him all. 'She said it would be better for me to be here. To raise our child on his own land.'

A sly argument. He would not know whether she was with child before he sailed.

He hesitated. 'But only until we reach Castile.' Determination in his eyes again. 'I will not fail you.'

Castile. Castile. She was sick to death of hearing that hated name. 'I know that.' Knew and despaired of being able to change his mind. 'Until then, perhaps I could create a corner of Castile here.'

'Impossible.'

'Something to remind us. My own sort of promise.' She must not let him tell her no. 'I thought a garden.' A garden she wanted as much as he longed for Castile. 'A garden like the one at Alcázar.'

'Alcázar has tiled courtyards and ponds with fish of gold and trees with fruit like the sun.'

She could create none of that. And he knew it. 'I had roses in Kent,' she said, quickly, 'and a quince tree that Eleanor brought with her from Castile…' No longer hers. None of it. 'Perhaps I can get a cutting from someone else's garden—'

'No. There will be no gardens here.'

No hope then. Both of them to be denied their dearest wishes.

They walked in silence and she let the shades of green comfort her. Even without a gardener's hand, there were sparks of colour, a few flowers too stubborn to die. At the edge of a stand of trees, she saw tall stalks of purple foxglove, reaching as high as her waist, waving in the breeze until she thought the bell-shaped blossoms would ring.

'See there?' she said, pointing. 'We do not need golden fish. The flowers on your own land are as pretty as any in Castile.'

He looked where she pointed, but instead of a smile, the waving wall of purple made him frown. 'Not pretty,' he said, staring at them. 'Poisonous.'

And when they returned, he told the steward to cut them all to the ground.

It was when they ran short of salt and the splintered shutters let the rain into the bedchamber that Gil was forced to admit his wife might be right.

The first nights had been only Gil and his wife and the wonder of discovery. The days, he barely noticed, though she tugged him into exploration of the keep and lands, showing him places he had not seen in years.

Lancaster had been right to chide him for neglect.

So, reluctantly, he began to review the status of his holdings and agreed that Valerie should continue the work while he sailed with the King. He did not want his child born here, but if a babe was to come, he would be back in time for those decisions.

So over the next week, he worked tirelessly

with the steward to repair the worst of the damage so that she could have some comfort.

In the meantime, Valerie focused on the land. Lancaster had laughed about her interest in the rye crop, but when she started asking pointed questions of the steward, Gil was impressed instead of amused.

He knew she loved flowers, but he discovered she had an aptitude for other growing things as well. The steward and some of the villeins were wary of her, true, but Gil made it clear they were to support her ideas. She spoke of beans and peas and why the yields were so poor and she asked whether barley for brewing might be a better choice for the south field.

In short, her conversation was as baffling to him as talk of men and weapons were to her.

He had never had an interest in such things. The Brewen men were warriors, not farmers. To Gil, the very earth the castle sat on seemed poisoned. But as he watched Valerie plan, he found himself wondering whether more fruitful land might have prevented his uncles from turning to robbery.

And worse.

Strange to be in the castle again. He had

been away so long that his memories had supplanted what stood before him. And now, days and nights with his bride were building new memories, ones he would want to think about in the coming months.

And so he tried to put the past aside, for a time, as he had asked her to do, layering new memories on top of the old.

Time and earth had covered most of them.

God willing, they would remain truly buried.

The days turned to August. Valerie had one night more, perhaps two, with her husband before she lost him to Lancaster, to war, to his dreams of glory. He would leave for London, where Katherine would join him, then they would ride on to the coast while Valerie would remain here, praying for a child.

She wanted a child in a way she never had before. Not just for herself or for her protection, but for him, so that he would know that his blood could create something wonderful. Then, perhaps, he would be truly able to overcome the past.

Perhaps he would even want to give a son the birthright of his land.

On that last summer day, while Gil supervised the mending of the courtyard well, she wandered beyond the walls, thinking of where she might situate a garden.

He was convinced they would not be here long enough, but he was going to allow her to stay, at least for a while. And so, she had begun to dream of a garden again.

No need to tell Gil her plans. She was not ready to begin, but only assess the earth. To judge what she might work with.

Outside the south wall, she paced off a small area, liking the way the sun fell on this side, and dreamt of another quince tree, that might, given years, blossom here. Her child might play in its shade some summer day like this one.

She had found a rake, missing some teeth, and a too-small trowel, and began digging in the earth, for the delight of it alone, for it was not a time for planting. A few mushrooms had sprouted, unfamiliar shapes, so she did not know whether they were safe to eat. The dirt seemed mounded here, as if the plot might have been used before, and she started raking the grass from the top, then, kneeling, dug with the trowel.

And hit something hard.

A rock, no doubt. She might have to pull

up several so that the earth could be prepared for seed. But the edge of the trowel slipped, as if there were a small rock, then hit something else. Maybe a pile of them?

She stood and picked up the rake again, alternately scraping and digging, trying to see what was there.

And when she cleared less than a foot of earth away, she saw, clearly, there were no rocks.

She had uncovered bones. Human bones.

Sunset was hours away when they finished repairing the shutters, but Gil was already wondering whether he might retire to the bedchamber with his wife unnoticed.

One more night.

If he had only himself to get to Dover, he might have tarried longer, but he had promised to escort Lady Katherine, which meant a longer journey and slower travel than with the men alone.

One more night with his wife.

She was nowhere to be found in the castle, but someone said she had gone beyond the walls and he followed, a strange sense of unease riding his shoulder. And when he turned the corner to the south side of the castle, he knew why.

She had uncovered all he had hoped would stay hidden. From her. From himself.

For she was staring down at the buried remains of Father Richard Brewen, the long-dead priest of Gadby Parish.

His wife looked up at him, eyes wide and dark.

'There was no stone. I did not know it was a grave.'

Crossing herself to ward off evil.

'It was not marked.' They had tried to hide it, so that no one would know, ever, what was there. How could he have been such a fool as to think the past would stay safely buried?

No, he had known the truth would come to light. He had just hoped…

She swallowed and stepped back, as if trying not to tread on the body. 'Who is it?'

'My uncle.'

'One of the Brewens?' Her tone, now, full of dread, as if she were beginning to suspect what that might mean.

He nodded. 'And a priest.'

Valerie dared to look back at the bones. A priest, buried in a hidden grave. She clenched a fist against her fears. It had been easy to forgive the past when it was safely out of sight, but in all his confessions, her husband had said nothing of this.

She raised her eyes to his. 'He did not die of old age.'

'No.' His expression, bleak. 'He was poisoned at his sister's table. And until now, I have been the only person alive who knew.'

Finally, she understood. Arrogant, she had dismissed his feelings, but now she saw the evidence in the earth and she, too, felt the crush of fear, the need to escape the family's sins. Every time he came home, every time he even thought of it, he faced a terrible secret.

A sister, killing a brother. A woman, killing a priest. And the murderer: his mother. What man would not want to leave it buried for ever?

He grabbed the trowel and started throwing the dirt back on top of the bones. 'I did not know where they had put him. The story was that he had visited and left late in the evening. No one ever saw him again.'

'Except you.' Without thinking, she picked up the rake to help him cover the bones again. How long had they lain undiscovered? 'When did this happen?'

'At the time of the Pestilence. One more death, even that of a priest...' He shrugged. 'No one questioned it.'

'But you were a child.' Twenty years ago at least. He could have been no more than six. Children did not always understand what they saw. 'You might be mistaken.'

He paused. 'I saw them that night, carrying the body out of the castle.' Gazing into the distance, as if seeing it all once more. And then, he picked up the trowel again. 'They sent me away after that, to Losford's service. And before I left, my mother told me to leave all I knew of the Brewens behind. I did not see her alive again.'

'But why?' All the woman's other brothers, outlaws. And yet, she would kill a priest. 'Why this man?'

'Because he was the one controlling all the rest. He was the Brewen directing the entire band.'

Fighting against corrupt churchmen, he had told her, when first he'd shared the tale. Perhaps there was some truth in that.

Gil patted down the earth and rose, reaching for some fallen branches, and threw them across the spot, to hide it again.

'I was wrong to come back, to think you

could stay here.' The look on his face brooked no argument. 'We leave at daybreak.' He hesitated, as if uncertain. 'And Valerie, please—'

'I will speak no more of this,' she said, sad that he felt he must ask. 'Ever.'

Chapter Seventeen

It was mid-August when Gil arrived at the coast with Valerie, Lady Katherine, and a small group of knights. It was a day of public prayers for the expedition.

They would be needed.

In the weeks Gil had been away, plans had changed again. Another French threat lay before them. The town of La Rochelle was under siege. The French and the Castilians had returned, blockading the port, trying to starve the residents into submission.

And so, the King declared they would sail back to the scene of June's defeat. This time, he vowed, it would be different. This time, they were prepared. Ships, men: enough to prove their might.

But to relieve the siege, they must land in Brittany, so sailing must be again delayed as

calls went out for the horses that had been ignored before since each knight must have at
least three horses to wage a land campaign.

King Edward had not yet arrived, but three
thousand men and three thousand archers
were gathering, along with pages, grooms and
other attendants who could not be counted.
They were to be put on nearly two hundred
ships, manned by five thousand sailors, and
led by the highest-ranking lords in the kingdom.

Military camps spread around the port
and beyond, spilling towards Dover, twelve
miles away. Lancaster had arrived and set up
a command tent. Lady Katherine joined him
quickly while Gil and Valerie travelled on to
Losford Castle, where he intended Valerie to
stay while he was at war.

They had spoken no more of the ghastly
discovery during their journey. Although she
had asked no further questions, neither had
her timid manner returned, so it seemed the
truth had not made her fear him. Instead, she
had an air of deliberate calm, as if she was
still processing the ghastly truth and trying
to decide what she might do.

The gates of Losford opened to them, more
welcoming, it seemed, than his own home.

Smiles. Introductions to his bride. But before all the greetings were complete, little Denys burst into the courtyard and ran up to him. 'Are you here to take me now?'

'Do not bother Sir Gilbert when he has barely crossed our threshold,' Marc said. 'We can discuss your fostering with him after he has had food and drink.'

As if it had been settled. As if they truly wanted to entrust him with their son.

Too late, he remembered they had expected him to ask Valerie about taking in Denys. But he had thought that merely a nicety, spoken to spare his feelings in front of the boy. He had thought that by now, they would have settled on someone else.

Someone more worthy.

Denys, crestfallen, dropped his head. His mother reached for him, pulling him against her skirts.

'I know he must go,' Cecily said to Valerie, 'but he is still so young. And to go directly to war...' Her hand tightened on the child's shoulder.

'If you do not think he can go to sea, I can take him back to Leicester with me to begin his training.' This was Valerie's voice.

All eyes turned to her.

'Allow me,' he said, quietly, 'to speak to my wife.'

They stepped out of earshot. Cecily put a hand on Marc's shoulder and they both turned away, as if they were not listening. Denys made no such pretence.

Gil frowned at Valerie, feeling his temper flare. 'Taking another woman's son will not bring you your own,' he said, shar and under his breath.

Her face crumbled at the hurtful words. Then, her calm expression returned, but with a new resolve he had not seen before. 'No. Only you can do that.'

He flinched at the blow. One he deserved. 'You cannot take him there. We will never return. Not now.'

'Return? You bring the place *with* you, carrying it on your back like a boulder that only you can see.'

The meek-tongued woman who had cowered at his every word was gone.

'You do not know the whole of it. When I was here in March, he was not so eager. Even Cecily hesitates to let him go with me. It is not your place to force him.'

'Force him? He cannot wait to go to war. And my offer would allow the boy to leave home without being in harm's way. Cecily might be content with that, though Denys will not. He would much rather sail with Sir Gilbert Wolford than languish in Leicestershire.' She paused and smiled. 'I suspect you were much like him when you came to Losford.'

When he came to Losford... He was younger than this boy, carrying the secret of his dead uncle, with everything to prove, most of all to himself. He owed Cecily's father everything. Cecily herself had been like a sister to him. How could he deny her anything? And even Marc—

He glanced at them. He could not read their faces.

Such a small boy to be sent away, not just to be fostered, but on a ship about to sail into war. He looked at Valerie, for a moment helpless. He had asked her for honesty. He could not complain when she gave it to him. 'You will not return, but stay here with Cecily. If his parents are willing, I will take the boy.'

He walked back to Cecily and Marc. 'So what have you decided?' Marc said.

'If you are certain it is what you want, he can come with me.'

Marc, enveloping him in a quick hug. Cecily, nodding while fighting tears. She had been born a countess. She knew what must be done.

Marc looked at his son. 'Do you want to go on the boat with Sir Gilbert? Are you ready?'

'A boat?' This time, there was no eagerness on the boy's face.

So it was as he had feared. Faced with the choice, the boy had lost his excitement.

Gil crouched before him, to look him in the eye. 'That's right, Denys.' The old doubts, still strong. 'We must cross the sea to get to war. Are you sure?' He would do Denys no favours by forcing him to follow a Brewen. The boy would be happier with some other knight.

Denys studied him, silent.

Gil rose. 'His answer is clear. You should find someone else. Someone who—'

'Yes!' The boy's voice, loud and resolute. 'I go to pack my things!' And he marched out of the courtyard, as if to battle.

'How soon?' Cecily said, her eyes following him.

'A fortnight, I think,' Gil said. 'Little more.'

In two weeks' time, he would be at war for who knew how long, with no certainty that he would even return. Later, the thought weighed on him as he led Valerie to the room Cecily had given them.

He needed no directions.

'You seem at home here,' she said.

More at home than in your actual home, she meant.

And with the comforts Cecily and Marc had created here, Valerie would be more comfortable than in his crumbling castle. 'It's the first place in which I thought I might be more than a Brewen.'

And, though he did not say, where he discovered why he would need to be.

'You are more than your name. You've a lifetime of honourable achievement all your own.'

He smiled. 'And you are a woman who is more than the meek wren you pretended to be. But tonight, I want to speak no more of any of these things. Tonight, I want to sleep on a well-stuffed mattress beside my wife.'

Pink touched her cheeks. They had a few more nights before he left. He intended to make the most of them.

One morning, the Countess—Valerie could not yet think of her as Cecily—invited her to tour the castle and grounds. Valerie lis-

tened, nodding, impressed with the size and
strength and beauty of Losford, and waiting
for the Countess to reveal the reason she had
arranged for a private conversation.

'Gil told me of your husband's death. I am
sorry.'

Valerie murmured something expected. Gil
had his secrets; she had hers.

'And I thank you,' Cecily continued, 'for
being willing to accept Denys. We asked Gil
months ago, but when we did not hear, we
thought, perhaps, you did not want the boy.'

Want the boy? Without a child of her own,
she would welcome one to foster. 'Of course
I do. If I had only known—'

She bit her lip. Their troubles were not to
be shared.

But Cecily nodded, as if she already knew
the truth. 'We told him to speak with you.
Taking in a boy, committing to his training as
a page, a squire, a knight…this is not something Gil alone can do. So when he said no,
we assumed…'

And she would let that presumption stand.
Gil's self-doubts were not for her to share.
'And I thought *you* thought I was not grand
enough to teach the son of a countess.'

They shared a laugh and Valerie felt a moment of connection with this woman. 'Gil says you and your husband are very happy.' Unsure whether she should have spoken so, but wondering whether there was something to be learned from this couple.

Cecily's smile was unexpectedly shy. 'We are, but the journey to happiness was long. You see, my plans for my future and the King's plans for me were very different.'

Valerie had been young when these two had wed and knew little of their story. 'You defied the King?' This seemed as impossible as mounting a horse and riding to *chevauchée*. Certainly, she had never believed she could refuse Lancaster's command to marry, though she had tried to delay it. 'Did you and your husband agree on what should be done?'

Again, her laughter. 'No. We did not.'

'Nor do we agree on…all things.'

Cecily did not ask more. 'And yet, telling the King of my desires was not the hardest part. The hardest part came before that. I had to change.'

Valerie knew she had changed. But Gil? Would he? Could he? 'How did you do it? What finally made you change?'

'I faced a choice,' she said. 'The time came when I was not brave enough to let him go, but only brave enough to do what I must to keep him.'

She made it sound simple. But this woman was rich and powerful, with land of her own. And Valerie could not tell Gil that he would lose her if he went to Castile.

Or could she?

The Countess must have seen the doubt in her eyes. 'What is it you fear?'

She started to answer with the things she had feared of old, but before she could open her mouth, she realised that she no longer feared her husband's anger, for he had proven himself kind. Nor did she fear falling in love with him, for it was too late to prevent that.

No, what she feared now was that if she told him she did not want a life in Castile, he would think she did not want a life with *him*. Why should she refuse Castile? Mayhap it was as wonderful as Gil believed. Maybe she would learn to love unending sun and court-yards dizzy with colour.

But unless Gil made peace with his past, it would follow them all the way to Iberia. For contrary to what she had expected in this marriage, it was his past, not hers, that threatened to tear them apart.

'What I fear,' she said, 'is the truth.'

* * *

During the days, Gil had left Losford to meet with Lancaster, working on final preparations. He had taken Denys with him, getting the boy accustomed to life at camp and to obeying him without question.

Finally, King Edward arrived and boarded his ship. Tomorrow, he would turn over the Great Seal, naming his grandson as keeper of the realm in his absence. The ships, finally, would sail for France to relieve the siege at La Rochelle.

On that final day, Gil walked with Valerie along the cliffs outside Losford and he showed her, in the distance, the boats, just up the coast, massing in preparation.

'Why must you go?' she asked.

'What?' Uncertain he had heard aright.

'You say you must go. Why?'

Now that the time was close, was she remembering what had happened the last time her husband went to war? 'Because I am in service to My Lord of Spain.'

'But you do not go to Spain, where you say you want to go, and still your life is his? To be put in jeopardy for any purpose he pleases?'

'It is not like that.' He heard his voice rising, a bad sign.

They walked a while in silence, but when he said no more, she began again. 'And when it is all over—what then?'

'You know the answer. When we take Castile, I will have an office in the court of the King.'

'An office.' She said it as if she did not know what it meant.

'Yes. Earl Marshal. Or even the High Constable.' In Edward's court, these positions were hereditary, not open to a man with Brewen blood. All would be different in Castile's court. A new king could name any man he chose...

'And what does the High Constable do?'

He had not thought her an ignorant woman. 'He commands all the royal armies.'

'But when you have retaken the throne, there will be no need for fighting. Then what will you do each day?'

What indeed? What did one do in the absence of war? There had been a few years of peace, nearly ten years ago, when they held the French hostages in England. Eager to prove himself, he did not enjoy that time. He might, he thought, feel different today. He would have a son to raise.

'Even if there is no war, we must be vigilant, ready, so that no one will dare attack.'

'And will you like that work?'

'Like?'

'Will you get up each morning excited to what may come that day?'

Her questions sounded simple, but they threw him off guard, forced him to put into words things that all men knew without saying. 'It will not matter if I like it. It is my duty.'

She stopped on the path, making him stop as well, and then she gathered his hands in hers. 'Why is duty so important?'

He opened his mouth, but the only word he could think to say was *because*...

Because a man was judged by how well he fulfilled his duty. Because once he had proven himself, been accepted, become important, no one would question him, ever again.

He met her eyes. 'It is difficult to explain.'

She squeezed his fingers. 'Try.'

What could he say? He needed that acknowledgment from other men that said he belonged. That he was admired. He had searched for it his whole life. From the Earl of Losford. From My Lord of Spain. Even from

Marc de Marcel, who had unhorsed him at a tournament all those years ago.

But that dream, the one he had been striving for, was even more important now. Now, he must prove himself so he could lay all at the feet of a woman he loved.

'Because in Castile, I will no longer be a Brewen.'

And the look in her eyes said he had disappointed her. 'You will still be a Brewen,' she said. 'Perhaps, finally, you will no longer care.'

He pulled his hand from hers and stroked her hair. 'I want you to be proud of me.'

'Oh, my husband, do you not know how proud of you I already am?'

Reassurance. The duty of a wife. And yet her doubts were evident in her questions. He had promised her Castile and given her a broken stone. Even now, she had no home, sheltered by the Countess because when he took her to the Castle of the Weeping Winds, the past, the awful past that lurked in the very ground, had risen up to haunt him.

'We have not had an easy marriage so far,' he began. Now he was the one who gathered her hands in his. 'But I know you share my dream. And I swear, I swear, I will not fail you. Nothing on earth is more important to me. Do you believe me?'

Something in her face changed. He could not decipher her expression, but he sensed a determination such as he had seen in men about to ride into battle. 'Yes. I do.'

Chapter Eighteen

Valerie had known that those days at Losford were a reprieve, a respite from everything behind and all that was to come. She had even tried to pretend they would go on like this always.

But the end had come. He would leave tomorrow.

The August night was warm, despite the breeze from the sea, and she waited for him in her room, having shed everything but her shift.

Behind her, the sound of the door. She turned.

Her husband, filling the frame. Blocking the light. She welcomed the flutter in her centre. Pulled the covers around her.

He stepped across the threshold. 'Tomorrow. My duty…'

He did not finish, but she knew. His duty. To his lord. To his dream. Unbreakable.

One did one's duty for one's lord because of obligation. Even fear.

Her duty as a wife had been the same. Obligation. Fear. Expectation. But never desire. Never joy. Until him.

The flutter, stronger now. She said nothing, but slipped off the bed and stood, letting the covers drop from her shoulders. Proud. Unafraid. No longer thinking of any man but this one.

'Tonight,' she said, 'is not a night of duty.'

No more words, then. He was with her in two strides, wrapping her in his arms. A kiss... Oh, a kiss.

No wonder Cecily and Katherine were willing to defy kings and conventions for this.

She did not fear his desire now, nor her own. Perhaps shared passion was needed to summon his seed, to make a child grow between them.

If that was so, then this, their last night, would be the one.

Now, in truth, she could give him her body and her love, but she could not, in the end, give him the truth.

Gil had *become* Castile. His goal had become the reason, he believed, that he was worthy of her love.

She could not send him to war rejecting what he fought for, because he would think she rejected him.

In the morning, he rose before dawn and dressed for war, while she put on a gown, the one that would grace his final image of her. The one he would remember until they met again.

'Would you rather return to the Queen's service?' he asked, when he was ready. 'I know Cecily will be glad to have you, but you might serve Castile, in my absence.'

She shook her head. 'If the Queen needs me, she will send word.' She looked at him, then, trying to set his face in her mind so that she could bring it out in all the lonely days to come. 'I have a gift for you.'

He started to protest, but then she raised her hand. 'I gave you no wedding present. You are going to war. We will not be together again—for a long time.'

She extended her arm and let the tippet at the end of her sleeve dangle. It almost touched the floor. She untied it and laid it across his palm. 'A scarf. A token.'

Not of some nameless woman, but of her own.

He closed his fingers over the white silk, tight as if he would never release it. 'If I die, I vow to you the only scarf I carry will be yours.'

The tears came quick and hot. Strange, that promise, but it meant more to her than their wedding vows. All this time, she thought she had wanted only a child. But he had wanted to give her something much more.

No, this man was not the one her first husband was. In fact, he was a man much more dangerous.

He was a man she would ache to lose.

They did not have another quiet moment before he left. Preparation was hurried, goodbyes rushed, Denys chattering with excitement and his parents fighting tears.

Within an hour, they were gone.

She stood with Marc and Cecily, watching the horses until she could see them no more.

'It is late in the season,' Lady Cecily said, frowning up at the sky as they turned back to the castle. 'The winds are strong.'

She said it with the assurance of a woman who had grown by the sea and knew its moods, just as Valerie knew the soil beneath her feet.

'Will they be all right?' Valerie said, as they turned away. Her husband, their son. So many dangers.

'Only God can say.'

I want you to be proud of me.

She would not be prouder if he died. And if he did, would anyone notice a broken rock in his pocket and a soiled scarf near his chest? No doubt they would be tossed by the side of the road.

'You were kind, Cecily, to offer to let me stay,' she began a few days later, after they had watched the ships sail into the strait, then out of sight. 'But I have decided to return to the Castle of the Weeping Winds.'

Cecily studied her for a moment. 'You have decided to be brave.'

She shook her head. 'I was not brave enough,' she said. 'I could not send him to war knowing that I believed in nothing he fought for. But when he returns, he must know. And I hope...'

She hoped they could face the truth of his

past together, just as they had joined to over-come hers.

Until that day came, she had a garden to plan.

The fleet had sailed, finally, at the end of August, but they could not best the sea.

Day after day, and then week after week, they battled contrary winds. Poor Denys, Gil discovered, was no sailor. Fortunately, there was little or nothing for the boy to do and Gil let him sleep below decks.

In fact, few of the tempest-tossed men could enjoy even a minute of the time at sea. They could do little but cling to the rail and pray for calmer waters and calmer bellies.

At dawn on the seventh day, the winds calmed and they made some progress east-wards through the Channel. The boy crept above decks with hollow cheeks, looking for all the world as if he had indulged in too much wine.

'Come here. Sit by me.'

Denys did, nearly falling over before he could lower himself with dignity. They sat in silence, watching the coast of England glide by.

'Have we reached the sea?' the boy said, finally.

So soon, he must learn disappointment. 'The winds have kept us within sight of England.' The sea, La Rochelle, still miles, days away.

Denys's expression was puzzled, but he nodded, his head wobbling with fatigue. 'I wish we could fly across the water.'

'Here,' Gil said. 'Put your head on my shoulder.'

Denys hesitated.

'There is no shame in being a poor sailor,' he said. 'I have seen the King himself desert the deck when the sea turns loathsome.'

The boy's smile was wan, but at least he gave one. 'I am no seaman, for all that I grew up in sight of the water.' Denys shook his head. 'I would rather face the enemy than the waves.'

'Was that the reason?' Gil remembered now how Denys had swung from excitement to reluctance. 'The reason you hesitated when your father asked if you were ready to come with me?'

Denys nodded, his head drooping on his neck. 'I thought it would shame you. My sickness.'

'Really? I thought it was…' All this time, he had assumed. 'I thought you wanted to be fostered with someone else.'

A puzzled face. 'But your family rode beside the King in France.'

Gil opened his mouth to argue and then stopped. It was true. 'Is that what they told you?'

The seasickness was fading, the boy finally bright-eyed again. 'And that you were trained by my grandsire.'

'Did they say nothing of the Brewens? Of their…misdeeds?' Rape, extortion, murder, things he could not mention in front of the child.

The boy shrugged, as if it all meant nothing. 'They were pardoned.'

They were pardoned. And yet, Gil had not pardoned himself.

'And I thought you didn't want to serve with a Brewen.' A strange admission to make to a child, but he had known what that meant when he was the age of Denys.

'I wanted to serve with *you*. You did not do those things.'

And, snuggled trustingly against Gil's side, Denys closed his eyes and slept.

The ship continued rocking, but not as

much as Gil's world. The burden he had carried each day of his life? Nothing to this child.

You did not do those things.

And yet, as a child younger than this one, he had taken all the guilt unto himself, feeling as if the knowledge alone made him culpable for crimes he did not commit.

Who could trust a seven-year-old to be wise?

And yet, as the years went on, it would be this boy who would pass down the stories. Stories that, instead of becoming more vicious, would become more benign. One day, they would be tales that could be told at bedtime without bringing nightmares.

And what had he done for all these years? Battled the past over and over again, as if by sheer force of will he could change it. And all the while, he was the only one on the field, clinging to a war that had faded from the memory of other men.

But he had waited, holding back from marriage, from everything, waiting to be redeemed, all this time, thinking that Castile, and only that, would transform the past as well as the future. Castile was a vision, a grail, the culmination of a dream that would,

finally, let him rest, let him say *that is enough.
Now, finally, I am worthy.*

Now, Castile was drifting beyond his grasp.
Not this year. Next? What if he never reached
it?

What if he did?

*You will still be a Brewen. Perhaps, finally,
you will no longer care.*

He thought he wanted to restore honour
to the name. In fact, he wanted to banish it.
Strike it from all history, particularly his own.
Then, he had imagined, a woman would look
at him and see a worthy knight, one who deserved her admiration and more.

Her love.

That was what he had waited for.

He reached for the white-silk tippet Valerie
had given him. Love was what he had. Now.
If only he had seen it.

The Channel winds, contrary, sent the silk
flapping. He looked at the land again. Men
on the shore on horseback could move more
quickly than the ships against this wind. They
would not reach La Rochelle in time. He knew
it, even if the King did not.

Stuffing the token back in his pouch, he
smiled. And what if they never reached Castile? What then?

Well, he thought, with a sense of surprise, there was a priest who had never received a decent burial.

It was mid-September before Valerie arrived at the Castle of the Weeping Winds. The steward, surprised to see her again, nevertheless greeted her as the lady of the manor, bowing, listening, even when she gave him specific instructions on the care of the bean crop.

Truth to tell, he seemed relieved to share the burden.

Ah, how things could change, when little between Valerie and her husband was actually different. On the surface at least, she was his wife and this house, this land, was her own.

Autumn was the time to plant roses, but she had no cuttings, no way to start anew. Instead, when she was not working on matters of the estate, she wandered the grounds, learning the earth and the light and listening for a song in the winds.

But knowing what lay buried beneath the dirt by the south wall, she stayed on the edge of the spot, averting her eyes, silently crossing herself against the sacrilege, learning, in those weeks, some of what had driven her husband to leave this place.

She was surprised to discover a medlar tree. Not her beloved quince, but from the same family. A sign, perhaps. Different plants, unfamiliar flowers, might spring from this earth. And even from the earth of Castile. She, like Gil, must make peace with the land of her childhood. She must be brave enough to leave her home behind, while he must have the courage to return to his.

She counted the days until the brownish fruit might be picked. October? November?

Would Gil be home by then?

The weeks passed and she heard no word from the sea. Had they landed in triumph? Marched across France to restore England's glory? Or had these ships, too, been set afire and sunk beneath the waters?

Without news she clung to the comfort of the rhythms of the earth, and the new place she had been planted, hoping that new life would come, as it always did, in the spring.

And hoping that Gil, too, would return.

For weeks, King Edward held on to hope, certain the winds would change, but by mid-October, the fleet had travelled no further

from their original port than men could have
ridden in four days on horseback.

Winter was coming. The season for war
had passed.

The King, hurling curses on the French,
abandoned the effort. The ships returned to
Sandwich. Thousands of dispirited soldiers
disembarked, Gil and Denys among them.

Still, Lancaster would speak of war and
new plans and all that must be accomplished
before the spring when they could sail again.
'We will return to France and cut through the
countryside as we have before. If my brother's health has returned, he, too, can join in
the battle.'

Words said more as prayer than fact. Gil
suspected that neither the ageing King nor
his sickly eldest son was fit to lead an army
again. Lancaster must know that, too, even if
he did not want to say it aloud.

'And with Portugal's help, attacking from
the west, we will reach Seville before midsummer.'

How many times had Gil heard such plans,
even made such plans suspecting they were
mad, yet holding back criticism as he chased
Lancaster's dream, having made it his own?

And as he listened to Lancaster again spinning ideas into the air, the truth crept in upon him. They might never retake the throne.

And he no longer cared.

But could his wife be truly content to stay in England?

I want to sleep in truth, he had told her. Yet he had not even known the truth. He had not been a brave man, striving for a worthy goal, but a coward, running from a patch of earth.

He thought, somehow, that she had recognised that, even when he had not.

Without waiting for Lancaster to finish, Gil rose. 'You are my liege and I owe you my service, but not today. Today I am going home.'

He turned his back and left the room without waiting for an answer.

Outside, in the courtyard, Denys smiled to be on solid ground. He had recovered with all the energy of a seven-year-old boy, playing at a swordfight with another page while he waited. And when he saw Gil, he ran up, full of smiles for what would come next. 'Where do we go now?'

'Home.'

Disappointment thrust out the boy's lower lip. Gil put a hand on his head. 'Not your home, Denys. At least, not for long.' He must gather Valerie and thereby give Cecily and Marc a brief glimpse of their son again. 'My home.'

Joy returned to his face. 'Are we going to the Castle of the Weeping Winds?'

'Yes.'

Home to see if he still had a home.

Chapter Nineteen

Valerie spent the waning days of autumn preparing the earth, covering the plants and praying that the winter would be kind and the spring early.

The steward had become her enthusiastic partner. Despite her initial impression, he was neither lazy nor slovenly, but after years of the master's deliberate neglect, he had become discouraged. And so the harvest, for the first time in years, was a celebration, blessed by the presence of the new lady in the Hall.

And when the cold settled in, they developed new plans for the fields and the castle, and he even listened to her extravagant hopes for a tunnel vine arbour.

Of the expedition, she heard no word at all. Had they landed? Did he live or was she again a widow?

One hope did die. Her monthly had come again. The seed Gil had planted had not taken root. There would be no babe.

And as the days became shorter and darker, she faced alone the fear that she might never be able to fulfil this one, ultimate, duty of a woman and a wife and give her husband the child they both so desperately wanted.

Finally, word came, a messenger sent from the Duke's nearby holdings. The expedition had failed. Not gloriously, not defeated in honourable combat, nor even disastrously as the previous ships, but simply frustrated by the contrary forces of nature, beaten down like a garden, pummelled by hail in midsummer.

Neither men nor ships were lost, but there was no word from her husband as the weeks went on. She counted days and miles. First, he would have gone to Losford and discovered she had flouted his desires. Then what? Had his duties kept him away? Or did he truly hate this land so much that he would abandon her along with it?

She had disobeyed him, directly, thinking they understood each other well enough now that he could accept that. Had she been wrong?

And then, one day, in the pale, watery sunlight of a November noon, she saw a man on a horse.

Too far to see his face, but she did not need to. Even from a distance, she recognised the way he held his shoulders. And wrapped around his neck, fluttering behind him like a banner, was her white-silk tippet.

Eager, she ran out of the gate, thinking when he saw her he would hurry, but he did not urge the horse to gallop, or even trot. Was he so reluctant to return?

Then as he came closer, she saw he did not ride alone, but led a horse-drawn cart, with little Denys sitting on the seat, hands on the reins.

She wanted to run to Gil, wrap him in her arms and not let him go, but she did not know his mind, so she sent men out to help him and in the bustle of a watched arrival, they embraced awkwardly.

'The boy is tired,' he said, lifting him off the seat. Indeed, he fell asleep in Gil's arms and they handed him to the servants to prepare a bed.

As Gil let go, his gaze went to her belly, looking for a sign. She shook her head.

'We will try again,' he whispered, flashing that magical smile that meant the trying was no hardship.

She looked away, her eyes on the cart, trying to hide a blush. The cart was piled with chests and weapons, and something sticking up that looked suspiciously like a branch.

'You wanted to create our own corner of Alcázar,' he began. 'And you told me these had come from Castile.'

Astonishment and tears mingled as two strong men picked up two hemp-covered bundles from the cart and laid them at her feet. She looked down at the familiar earth of Kent and she recognised one of her rose bushes, now bare of flowers, bundled up with a sack of dirt, and transported halfway across England.

And beside it, a cutting from the quince tree.

She laughed, giddy. 'How did you get these?'

'I persuaded the new owner to part with them. And…' he pulled her favourite trowel from the cart '…something else I thought you might want.'

She reached for it, recognising the dirt still clinging to the edges. Such a commonplace thing. To see it, no one would know what a treasure he had given her.

But Gil did.

She blinked back tears as she took it from him. Gil was not crying. His smile, now broad and gentle, showed her that he understood, exactly, what it meant to her.

He pulled her closer and pressed a kiss to the top of her head. 'I love you.' A whisper. Only for her ears.

And as her tears spilled over, she flashed him a smile, magical, as promising as the ones he had shared. A smile that said, *Tonight, when we are alone, I will show you how much I love you, too.*

The next day, Valerie proudly guided him through the castle, then they walked much of the land, side by side, and he marvelled at all she had done. He complimented her on the larder, full and ready for winter, and he was interested, or pretended to be, in her plans to plant wheat where the beans had grown in past years.

But as they approached the site of the priest's bones, his steps slowed.

She took his hand, threading her fingers with his. She had disobeyed his wishes, forcing him to return to this place he hated, convinced he must make peace with his past.

How arrogant it seemed now, to insist that

he unearth the most haunted part of his past. She glanced at him, trying to gauge his mood, but held her tongue.

Only a few months since they had dug up the ground and covered it again, but the mushrooms had returned. Dead leaves had drifted over the spot. A cold winter? A wet spring? All would be hidden again.

The earth was resilient.

And he stood, in the sunny spot where the secret lay buried, and stared at it for a long time.

'An outlaw,' he said, finally, clearing his throat to let the words free, 'should not be buried in consecrated ground.'

She waited, hoping he would say more. Could he ever be at home here, knowing the past lay close beneath his feet?

'Perhaps we should just let him stay buried here.' And then he looked at her. 'I think you said this would be a good spot for a garden.'

She wrapped his arm in hers, tightly. 'Yes. Yes, it would.' New growing things to cover the vestiges of the past. 'A quince tree here—' she pointed '—and an arbour of roses against the wall. We can build a lattice. And later, perhaps a bench…'

Extravagant plans already. She glanced at him, wondering whether he would approve.

And saw him draw a familiar, battered stone from his pocket and hold it in his palm.

Castile. Still.

Then she, too, must make her peace. And learn the flowers of a sunnier clime.

She reached for her matching piece and held it next to his. Worn and broken, the two no longer fitted perfectly together, but the pattern of the tile was still clear.

'Lancaster will try again for the throne,' he said. 'There will be another expedition to Castile.'

The hard reality of the stone he carried. 'And you will go.' There could not be a question. It was his duty.

He nodded. 'But I think now, if you agree, that I will not want to stay.'

If she agreed. But she did not want to force her desires on him, any more than she had wanted to be forced into his. 'But it is everything you have ever wanted…'

'You have taught me to want something else. You. This. Can this be enough for you?'

He had asked for truth and she had been a coward. 'I was afraid to tell you before. I do not, I have *never* longed for Castile.'

A moment of confusion. 'But you are Castilian.'

'My ancestor was. But she came more than one hundred years ago! I can have no more than a drop of Castilian blood in my veins.'

'But you were so angry, when the invasion was cancelled.'

'Because of La Reina. She and I…' She did not know how to explain. 'She wanted to go home. I understood that.' They had shared the pain of being kept apart from the land that was theirs. 'But my home is with you now. No matter where you choose.'

'Here. I choose here. With you.'

She took the stone from his hand and crouched close to the earth. 'When the garden is done, we will place our stones in it.' She tucked them on top of the dirt. 'Side by side.'

A smile. Relaxed. Genuine. 'That will be all of Castile we ever need.'

Epilogue

Yuletide, 1372

Bertram Blount, steward of Wolford's Castle of the Laughing Winds, surveyed the Great Hall with pride.

The castle's name was not the only thing that had changed since the master's wife had come home. For the first time since Bertram had been steward, Yuletide was being celebrated with feasting. The stables were filled with the horses of visiting guests, minstrels strolled the Hall and the smell of roast boar filled the air.

His time here did not stretch back far enough to know the history behind the sadness that had gripped the place, though he had heard rumours. Tonight, the old ones, those who could remember the Brewen years, shook their heads and clucked their tongues.

You can never foresee, they said in whispers, *what miracles God may work.*

Certainly, he thought, Lady Valerie was among them.

She was calm, steady, but forceful as well. A woman, he thought, who had lived through some hard lessons and learned from them. And the master himself? Whatever sadness had touched him was largely gone. Once, twice, Bertram had seen the man look mournful, so he directed the cook to refrain from adding mushrooms to the stew. Everyone knew they could bring on melancholy.

But usually, Sir Gil was content. And when he looked at his wife, well, you seldom saw such a smile on a man unless he was in the bedchamber and…

Well, not to be mentioned in company. Surprising the lady was not yet with child, though little Denys was a handful.

The doorkeeper approached. 'A visitor,' he whispered. 'A monk, seeking shelter.'

'Let him enter. I'll inform the master.'

'Stay here,' Gil whispered to his wife, as he rose to follow the steward. 'I'll see to him.' Strange, for a monk to be wandering alone at Yuletide.

'Make him welcome,' his wife said. 'We've food aplenty if he is ready to break his fast.'

'Perhaps he became lost,' the steward said, as they walked to the small entry chamber by the gate.

But when Gil saw the monk, he knew the man was not lost. Though he had not seen him in more than twenty years, he recognised the pale blue eyes and the scar he had left on his brother's cheek when a childish fist-fight got too serious.

'Gilbert.' The monk looked at him, as if witnessing an apparition. 'So it is true. I had to come, to see for myself.'

'Michael.'

'Brother Michael now, but, yes.'

Gil said no more, but enfolded his brother in his arms and, for long minutes, neither moved nor spoke.

'I thought the place abandoned,' his brother said, when they finally separated to stare at each other again.

'It was. Or that was my intention.'

He heard the rustle of skirts behind him as Valerie entered, looking from one to the other. He reached for her hand. 'But something changed. Everything changed.'

The monk made the sign of the cross. 'After

all these years, God answered my prayers. He redeemed our family.'

Gil smiled. Some things, things his brother had been too young to know, were beyond redemption. But they had not been Gil's sins. Nor Michael's.

'Valerie, this is my brother Michael.'

'Come in,' she said. 'Welcome home.'

* * * * * *

*If you enjoyed this story,
you won't want to miss the other books
in Blythe Gifford's*
ROYAL WEDDINGS *trilogy*

*SECRETS AT COURT
WHISPERS AT COURT*

Author's Afterword

In my two previous books, *Secrets at Court* and *Whispers at Court*, I explored royal matches made for love: the stuff of romance and—we hope—happily ever after.

This book shows the more typical scenario: royal marriages made solely for political/ dynastic reasons.

Secrets at Court revolved around the marriage of Edward III's first son, also Edward, and *Whispers at Court* centred on the marriage of his oldest daughter, Isabella.

John of Gaunt, Duke of Lancaster, My Lord of Spain, was the third surviving son of King Edward III. Edmund, who married Constanza's sister, was the fourth son. Lancaster had, by all accounts, been deeply in love with his first wife, Blanche, before she died, but he would never be King of England, so when he had the chance to marry the heir to the throne of Castile, he took it.

Katherine Swynford, too, is a real historical figure and her affair with John began about this time, according to the best accounts available. Their love story, immortalised in Anya Seton's novel *Katherine*, continued for the rest of their lives. After Queen Constanza died Katherine and John were married and their four children were legitimised.

As always, I had to take a few liberties, streamline a few parts of the story and make my own decisions when historical reports were unclear or contradictory.

It was not only Castile, but Castile and Leon's throne that John claimed. Katherine Swynford did care for John's children from his first marriage, but the time she spent serving Constanza was probably much shorter than I have suggested here. She was probably not present at the birth of Catherine—the date of which is open to dispute—nor at the wedding of Isabel and Edmund. Indeed, her sister Philippa, who was married to the poet Geoffrey Chaucer, probably served La Reina for longer. And Chaucer's poem, *The Book of the Duchess*, was written about Blanche, the Duchess of Lancaster, so loved by John, her husband.

There is a difference of opinion about Constanza's ease with the language of England, but it has been generally agreed that she did not mingle with the rest of the court and kept largely to herself. Her sister, Isabella, had a quite different character, as I've described. I've called her Isabel, since the royal bride in *Whispers at Court* was also Isabella.

On the other hand, some of the most surprising details are true. Katherine Swynford *was* the messenger who brought news of the birth of the next heir to Castile's throne to King Edward III. The military situation that year was ever-changing—so quickly that it was hard to keep track—and when the fleet did sail, finally, for France, it was kept at bay for six weeks because of contrary winds and never made it across the Channel. And Constanza's mother was, indeed, her father's mistress and their 'marriage' the subject of some conjecture.

Though Valerie is my own creation, the story of her ancestor from Castile might easily have happened. The original Castilian Queen, Eleanor of Castile, who married Edward I, *did* bring her ladies with her and made certain many of them married Englishmen. She, too, had an avid interest in gardens and brought several Iberian gardeners to England, who introduced features often found in Islamic gardens, such as those at Alcázar.

Finally, the story of Gil's outlaw Brewen family was modelled on the Folvilles of Leicestershire—who, legend has it, did indeed kill a priest.

The Duke of Lancaster returned to fight in France the following year, though his 'Great Chevauchée' was a near disaster. Nearly a third of his men were lost to battle, accident, illness or desertion. I choose to be confident that Sir Gil Wolford and Denys came home safely.

The battle for Castile, and for France, continued for years beyond this story, which was just one episode in what came to be known as the Hundred Years War.

An expedition to conquer Castile was finally mounted in the mid-1380s, but before the end of the decade Lancaster had signed a treaty, giving up all claims to the country's kingship.

Ultimately John never sat on a throne, but his descendants did. His daughter with Blanche married into the Portuguese royal family and became Queen of Portugal. Catherine, his daughter by Constanza, whose birth is described in this book, married into the Castilian royal family and became Queen of Castile as part of a treaty in which 'My Lord of Spain' and Constanza gave up their own claim to the throne.

John, most historians agree, did *not* have designs on the throne of England. But within a few years his descendants, called the Lancastrians, did sit on the throne. Henry IV, his son with Blanche, was the first Lancastrian King and his son and grandson—Henry V and Henry VI—reigned after him. The War of the Roses was fought between the descendants of John, Duke of Lancaster, and those of Edmund, Duke of York, whose wedding to Isabel we see in this story.

And as for the first Tudor King, Henry VII—the King who reunited the Lancaster and York factions after the War of the Roses—he was descended from John and Katherine's son John, with whom she is pregnant in this book.

Finally, the closest language to medieval Castilian is present-day Spanish. Please forgive any errors in my translation.

MILLS & BOON®

HISTORICAL

AWAKEN THE ROMANCE OF THE PAST

A sneak peek at next month's titles...

In stores from 1st June 2017:

Just can't wait?
Buy our books online before they hit the shops!
www.millsandboon.co.uk

Also available as eBooks.

MILLS & BOON®

EXCLUSIVE EXTRACT

Desperation forces Georgiana Wickford to
propose to her estranged childhood friend.
The Earl of Ashenden swore he'd never wed,
but the unconventional debutante soon tempts
him in ways he never expected!

Read on for a sneak preview of
THE DEBUTANTE'S DARING PROPOSAL

Georgiana couldn't really believe that his attitude could
still hurt so much. Not after all the times he'd pretended
he couldn't even see her, when she'd been standing
practically under his nose. She really ought to be immune
to his disdain by now.

'Did you have something in particular to ask me,'
Edmund asked in a bored tone, 'or should I take my
dog, and return to Fontenay Court?'

'You know very well I have something of great importance to ask you,' she retorted, finally reaching the end
of her tether as she straightened up, 'or I wouldn't have
sent you that note.'

'And are you going to tell me what it is anytime
soon?' He pulled his watch from his waistcoat pocket
and looked down at it. 'Only, I have a great many
pressing matters to attend to.'

She sucked in a deep breath. 'I do beg your pardon,
my lord,' she said, dipping into the best curtsey she

could manage with a dog squirming round her ankles and her riding habit still looped over one arm. 'Thank you so much for sparing me a few minutes of your valuable time,' she added, through gritted teeth.

'Not at all.' He made one of those graceful, languid gestures with his hand that indicated *noblesse oblige*. 'Though I should, of course, appreciate it if you would make it quick.'

Make it quick? Make it quick! Four days she'd been waiting for him to show up, four days he'd kept her in an agony of suspense, and now he was here, he was making it clear he wanted the meeting to be as brief as possible so he could get back to where he belonged. In his stuffy house, with his stuffy servants, and his stuffy lifestyle.

Just once, she'd like to shake him out of that horrid, contemptuous, self-satisfied attitude of his towards the rest of the world. And make him experience a genuine, human emotion. No matter what.

'Very well.' She'd say what she'd come to say, without preamble. Which would at least give her the pleasure of shocking him almost as much as if she really were to throw her boot at him.

'If you must know, I want you to marry me.'

Don't miss
THE DEBUTANTE'S DARING PROPOSAL
by Annie Burrows

Available June 2017
www.millsandboon.co.uk

Join Britain's BIGGEST Romance Book Club

50% OFF your first parcel

- **EXCLUSIVE offers** every month
- **FREE delivery direct** to your door
- **NEVER MISS a title**
- **EARN Bonus Book** points

Call Customer Services
0844 844 1358*

or visit
hillsandboon.co.uk/subscriptions

* This call will cost you 7 pence per minute plus your phone company's price per minute access charge.

MILLS & BOON®
are delighted to support
World Book Night

Georgie Lee

The Secret Marriage Pact

www.millsandboon.co.uk

WB0517_2